Contents

Dedication

This story is dedicated to all of those who seek comfort in the bright stars of the night and in the whispers of the wind, a gift to those who have felt lost in the immensity of the universe, but have found solace in the mystical beauty that resides within ourselves and around us.

May this journey full of magic and mystery in the depths of the human soul. Awaken your wonder and inspire you to discover the infinite power that lives within our souls. May we learn to appreciate the perfection that hides within the enigmas of life and that we find the courage to face uncertainties, losing ourselves in the enchanting romance between reality and fantasy.

Acknowledgements

To my very life, my beloved cat, whose constant presence has enriched every day of my existence with happiness and unconditional affection, showing me the purest expression of eternal love.

To my chosen family and my dear friends, the lanterns that light my way.

To the majestic nature and the breathtaking beauty of our planet, which has always inspired me, and with every awakening, has nourished my spirit and enriched my soul.

To the vast universe, for its deep mysteries and spectacular wonders, for the lessons and blessings. In every star in the skies, in every gust of wind, and in every beat of my heart, I have found the magic and wisdom I have been searching for.

To the readers, may your curiosity and passion for discovering new realities bring these pages to life. May this literary journey transport you to a world full of imagination and introspection, and may it bring answers to the questions that overwhelm us on our journey through this earthly plane.

About The Author

J.D. Pujals (born May 16, 1984, in Santo Domingo, Dominican Republic) is a multifaceted Canadian artist. Renowned as a painter, sculptor and writer, his work reflects a fusion of the figurative and the abstract, infused with a mystical touch and a deep connection with nature.

From an early age, he showed an innate inclination toward art and writing, exploring the intersections between the human mind, the universe, and magic. His literary style, inspired by Latin American magical realism, is characterized by its relaxed, casual, and lighthearted tone, which invites internal reflection and the search for each individual's purpose in life.

J.D. Pujals' educational and professional background is as diverse as his art. At the age of 6, he moved to the United States, where he was exposed to a new culture and outlook on life. This early experience enriched his worldview and contributed to the formation of his artistic identity. Subsequently, he returned to the Dominican Republic to continue his studies. He graduated with a degree in advertising, a discipline that, along with his exposure to Dominican culture, influenced his understanding of visual communication and storytelling, aspects that he would later integrate into his art.

Following his training in advertising, he ventured to Chile, where the region's rich cultural diversity and artistic effervescence further stimulated his creativity. He decided to study industrial design in Spain, thus exploring a new aesthetic and conceptual dimensions that would be reflected in his work. After completing his training, he returned from Spain to Chile, where he worked as a teacher of English as a second language for several years, working for one of the largest pharmaceutical companies in the world.

He later moved to Canada, where he currently lives. He is deeply influenced by the landscapes, cultural diversity, and society's commitment to environmental protection and animal rights. This experience marked a significant change in his life, leading him to adopt a plant-based lifestyle, which he incorporates into his writings through a strong message of environmental awareness and respect for all forms of life.

His art has been exhibited and recognized internationally, highlighting its ability to evoke emotions and awaken people's imagination. His commitment to exploring the human soul and promoting happiness and fulfillment is reflected in both his art and his words, demonstrating that the true purpose of life lies in living in harmony with oneself and the world around us.

J.D. Pujals' work transcends borders and cultures, inspiring others to seek beauty and meaning in every moment of life and the magic all around us.

Epigraph

"On the journey of existence, the threads that connect our dreams to reality are often entwined, guiding us through a path of awakening, hidden messages, and the deep connection between the ordinary and the extraordinary."

Preface

Maple, an artist and a dreamer, always felt a deep connection to the world around her. Her passion for nature and her love for animals led her in search of a deeper meaning and to explore the mysteries of a cosmos that seemed to whisper secrets in her ear. Her life, a puzzle of strange experiences, enigmatic symbols and the charm of Marina Willows Park, her precious sanctuary.

At the most unexpected moment of her existence, Maple found herself at the intersection of an ordinary life and an extraordinary destiny. This is the story of her odyssey, which soaked her in magic, and transported her from an ordinary life to an extraordinary one.

Maple stumbles upon a series of hidden messages, symbols, and mysterious voices that echo in her mind. A chance encounter in the woods triggers a series of events that forever alter the course of her life. She embarks on a quest to uncover the hidden truths of her destiny, guided by a being of unimaginable power: a being who personifies all that exists.

Maple's journey is marked by experiences both fantastical and profound as she navigates complex relationships, from her complicated family dynamics to the unbreakable support of her chosen family and friends, all while dealing with the profound questions about her destiny.

While enjoying success on social media, Maple uses her platform to inspire, educate, and spread love and positivity.

Yet the ever-present mysteries of her past continue to call her in murmurs she cannot ignore.

In this story of self-discovery, connection, and transformation, Maple's awakening is a reminder that life's most extraordinary adventures often lie just beneath the surface of the ordinary. This is a story about the power of dreams, the beauty of nature, and the call of a universe eager to reveal its wonders to those willing to open their eyes.

Join Maple on her adventure, guided by the mysterious hand of destiny, as she learns that the greatest secrets of the universe lie at the surface of our own selves. Get ready to embark on a magical odyssey that transcends reality and illuminates the power of hope, love, and the human spirit.

Introduction

Maple Pelridge, with her curly red hair like fire, and her blue eyes as deep as the ocean, is a woman as special as the amazing landscapes that surround her. In the middle of a charming little city in the northwest of the Pacific Ocean, known for its abundant vegetation and its serene atmosphere, Maple was ready for something new.

Maple's story is one full of contrasts: dreams and reality, laughter and tears, love and loss. At 39, she was trapped in the monotonous routine of a meaningless job, a job that turned off her vibrant essence. Yet in her heart burned a flame of unwavering optimism.

Maple loved animals, beyond mere affection. Pancake, her dog, was the center of her universe, and her lifestyle was a passionate commitment to ending animal suffering. She felt such deep compassion that she couldn't even hurt a fly.

Nature was undoubtedly her sanctuary. She frequently ventured into the woods, discovering trails in the mountains, and scattering wildflower seeds, in hopes of bringing color and life to the world she adored so much.

Her home was a cozy retreat full of creativity and dreams, shared with her quiet roommate, Ria.

Ria, an old soul despite her short 24 years, complemented Maple's vibrant personality with her own quiet strength and passion for the small pleasures of life.

Maple was not only friends with Ria, but she was also like a mother figure.

Maple's best friend since childhood, Julie, was a constant source of inexhaustible support. Their friendship, built on years of shared secrets and mutual understanding, was a beacon of light in Maple's sometimes turbulent world.

Maple's family life was also complex. Her younger sister, Honey, had a sarcastic humor and a straightforward demeanor, which contrasted sharply with Maple's dreamy nature. Despite their differences, they shared a deep bond, which they didn't always recognize. Her mother, Pearl, and her spouse, Lars, gave her valuable advice and inspired her to keep going forward.

The loss of her father, Roman, left an indelible mark on Maple's heart. She worried that she would not be able to give her beloved mother a comfortable life.

In the midst of her complex web of relationships and emotions, Maple's dreams soared high. She longed to leave her mark on the world, share her dreams of life, nature, and the universe. Her artistic soul found comfort in art, transforming ordinary things into treasures full of secrets waiting to be deciphered.

This is the amazing story of Maple Pelridge, a story full of resilience, compassion, and the tireless search for our purpose as living beings sharing this beautiful planet called Earth.

Chapter 1: Maple

Maple's soul was truly unique, without a doubt. Small freckles adorned her face, like sparks left by a comet. What really set Maple apart, however, was her endless optimism. A sense of humor with the ability to make the angriest souls smile.

Maple had a great passion for animals. Her greatest treasure was a dog named Pancake. Maple did not consider herself a simple pet enthusiast, for Maple, Pancake was her entire universe. She followed a plant-based lifestyle not only for health reasons, but as a passionate commitment to ending the injustices suffered by animals in the food industry.

Maple's love of nature often led her to explore the world around her by hiking and mountain climbing. She had even embarked on a personal mission to scatter native wildflower seeds during her walks, hoping to make a more beautiful world for all the creatures that inhabit the earth.

Maple resided in a cozy apartment in an old building in the center of the city. The city itself was an epitome of old-world charm, with lush greenery and right on the edge of an amazing park.

Her roommate, Ria, was an old soul trapped in a young body, she possessed a sharp mind, a passion for reading, and love for the flute, which she played very discreetly in her room or very passionately in the nearby park.

When the colder months came, her skillful fingers found solace in the art of knitting. At 24, she possessed a fascination with numbers, languages, a love of classical music, and a keen curiosity for online strategy games. Her quirks painted a portrait of her unique personality.

Maple's role in Ria's life was part maternal and part sister-like. The age difference between them allowed for a unique dynamic of support and friendship.

Maple's best friend Julie had been a constant presence in her life since childhood. Their friendship was an unbreakable bond forged over the years. Julie was a sweet and honest soul. She had short, curly hair that framed her face. Her radiant hazel eyes shone with warmth and her bright smile could brighten up the darkest days.

Julie wasn't just a best friend; she was Maple's confidant. She knew the deepest secrets of Maple's childhood and the scars that had been etched in her heart.

Julie's appearance defied societal standards of beauty. She had a beautiful, tanned complexion and a smile that could melt even the coldest of hearts. Maple appreciated her authenticity and unbreakable support as a precious gift. Julie's mother, Dinorah, was a therapist who used puppets in her sessions. She had a unique bond with her daughter, Julie, though some would say it was too close for comfort.

Julie was engaged to Sam, a man she had been dating since they went to high school together. Sam was an extraordinary person, a lawyer with a successful career, great wealth, and a sharp mind. Their relationship was based on love and friendship, although they no longer felt the burning passion of their youth.

Although Julie and Sam loved each other deeply, Julie couldn't escape the persistent doubt about Sam's ambiguous preferences. It was a source of insecurity that Julie had carried with her for years.

Maple often advised Julie to take a break from her long relationship with Sam, to discover herself as an individual. But Julie was afraid of being alone, and her answer to many dilemmas was a simple "I don't know."

Honey, her sister, was quite different in every way. She was tall, 5'8", her presence was strong and confident. Honey's sarcastic and dry humor aligned with her realistic outlook on life. Her hair, dyed a deep magenta, contrasted with Maple's red locks, and it was perfectly straight, as was her sense of humor. Despite their differences, Honey and Maple shared a deep connection, one they didn't always know how to recognize.

Maple's life was a dichotomy between dreams and reality. At 5'9" tall, she had aspirations that rose above the mundane. However, at 39, she found herself stuck in a dead-end job at a call center, a position that drained her soul with each passing day. Her younger sister, Honey, was her boss at the call center, which made Maple feel like a total failure.

Every shift at the call center felt like a lost moment, a reminder of unfulfilled dreams. Boring, monotonous conversations with annoying customers left her wanting something more, something to ignite her spirit. The reality is that Maple didn't care about this job; it wasn't her passion; she knew she was destined for something greater.

Maple's dreams weren't limited by the walls of the call center. She longed to be an online influencer, to create a digital space that would resonate in the hearts of many. She wanted to share her thoughts on life, nature, animals, love, friendship, the universe, and our deep connection to it all. It wasn't about fame or ego; It was all a matter of reach.

However, there was an obvious obstacle in her way. The cruel reality of the digital world was that influence often equaled the number of followers. With only a few hundred followers on her social media accounts, her content barely made a splash in the vast ocean of the internet.

Maple was a creative woman, but the call center drained her energy, making it difficult to unleash her artistic prowess. A painter, sculptor, and artist in every sense of the word, crafts were an incredible stress reliever for her. When inspiration struck, she painted rocks with secret messages, hiding them all over the city so that unsuspecting walkers would find them.

Mysticism held a special place in Maple's heart. She believed in a higher power, a force that connected all living things. However, she was not bound by the confines of religion, as her faith transcended the boundaries of dogma.

Her childhood had been anything but perfect. Trauma had left its mark, and her relationship with her parents, Pearl and Roman, was far from being simple. Roman, her father, had passed away after a long battle with kidney cancer the previous year. He was a loving father with an abundance of good advice. Unfortunately, his priorities as a father and as a man were not always in the right place.

Maple's parents had divorced, a decision driven by Roman's countless romances throughout their 18-year union. Pearl, Maple's mother, was a kind soul. Her friendly and docile nature had attracted Lars, a man who had become her devoted spouse for years. Honey harbored no affection for Lars, believing that Lars would never be able to fill her father Roman's shoes. Lars' loud personality often overshadowed Pearl's soft light.

Although Lars was a talented artist, he had financial problems, and his talent was overshadowed by his financial instability. Maple admired Lars for his talent, but she couldn't help but feel that he could never truly replace her father, Roman.

However, the love between Pearl and Lars was undeniable. Pearl had been a devoted spouse who took care of the house, first with Roman and now with Lars. She had spent her life caring for them, nurturing their hearts, and supporting their dreams.

Doris, Maple's only living grandmother, was a thread of continuity in her life. At 98, Doris had dementia, and her memories had become fragmented pieces of a life well lived that once was.

Maple had always longed for a brother, as her connection to Honey had never truly blossomed in her eyes. She once heard whispers about a long-lost brother, a product of Roman's adventurous heart. This information had led Pearl to file for divorce.

Maple's financial troubles had begun when her relationship with Jonah ended. He was a kind and genuine man, a dreamer with boundless creativity. However, Jonah's tendency to live in a fantasy world clashed with Maple's desire to have a partner with clear goals in life. Jonah's mental health had been a recurring challenge during their time together. He had been admitted to a mental hospital six times in a single year, a battle that had taken its toll on both of them.

It became too much for Maple, and she decided to end their romantic relationship. They remained friends, but the pain of separation had led Jonah to return to his parents' hometown. Then Jonah disappeared, leaving no trace of his online presence.

Maple worried about him, wondering where he might be. However, she had decided to move on, focusing on her dreams of becoming an online influencer.

Chapter 2: The First Contact

One Wednesday morning, while strolling through her favorite park, Marina Willows, a vast and diverse green space, Maple felt an inexplicable urge to go pick some berries. A voice inside her told her to visit a wooded part of the park known for its extraordinary charm that Maple affectionately called "Fairy Forest" even though people called it the Enchanted Forest. The voice Maple heard was her own, a thought that echoed in her mind. It was her day off, so she decided to answer the call of the mysterious voice. Maple had always been on a quest to lose weight. She was on a diet of vegan berry smoothies, not only for her physical health, but also for the boost they provided to her overall mood. The weight loss plan filled her with motivation and a firm belief that she could make her dreams come true.

When Maple entered the "Fairy Forest, ", she felt as if her body was being guided down a specific path by an otherworldly force. It was as if an invisible hand was guiding her, and she followed without asking. She had been to this part of the park a million times before, but these trails seemed new and enchanting. With each step, Maple's senses sharpened, attuned to the extraordinary.

Maple's journey through the dense forest was filled with anticipation and a sense of wonder. As she navigated the labyrinthine paths, the rustle of leaves and the soft crunch of the twigs under her feet intensified the mystical atmosphere that surrounded her. The forest seemed to vibrate with an otherworldly energy, guiding Maple into the unexpected.

Finally, her wanderings led her to a clearing where there was a bush of white berries that emitted a soft, ethereal glow under the dappled sunlight. The sight was mesmerizing, and Maple couldn't help but be drawn to the magical aura emanating from the berries. They seemed to throb with an energy that transcended the real world. And Maple thought she heard a voice whispering to her to come a little closer.

However, Maple's excitement was tempered by a cautious conscience. She was well aware of the potential dangers lurking in nature. Consuming unknown berries could be dangerous, as they could be poisonous, and pose a serious risk to one's health. Despite the allure of the white berries, Maple hesitated, her survival instincts urging her to approach with caution. Standing in front of the white berry bush, Maple weighed in the temptation of the mystical fruit in the face of potential risks. The dichotomy between curiosity and prudence danced in her mind, adding an extra layer of complexity to her already enigmatic circumstance. The soft glow of the berries seemed to draw her in, provoking her with temptation, but Maple remained firm in the knowledge that not all that glitters is gold. Her decision at this crucial moment would set the course for the rest of her adventure, and the consequences of her choice hung in the air like the palpable magic surrounding the white berry bush.

Despite the warnings of her common sense, Maple could not resist the temptation. She plucked a small velvety white berry from the bush, and curiosity took possession of her. She took a small bite and immediately discarded the rest.

Fortunately, she suffered no immediate adverse effects. The berry tasted like any other berry she had ever tasted. She scolded herself for taking that risk and decided it was time to go home, but first she took a little memento of her almost magical experience.

When Maple arrived at her apartment, Pancake, her faithful dog, was waiting patiently at the door, wagging his tail happily, looking at Maple straight in the eye, with great intensity.

Suddenly, for reasons she couldn't comprehend, tears welled up in Maple's eyes. She felt a surge of emotion, overwhelmed by the injustice of life. She wished Pancake could talk, that he could communicate his thoughts and feelings to her, but all he could offer were his silent, loving eyes. Maple looked around the place she called home.

Her apartment, full of brightness, reflected her vibrant personality. It was adorned with numerous plants and mirrors that reflected her own soul. When Maple looked at herself in one of the many mirrors, it was as if she was experiencing an out-of-body moment. Maple's reflection in the mirror said out loud, in Maple's own voice, "You are Sky, you are Water."

Suddenly, the smart speaker in the kitchen said: Ok Maple, here's Sky Water. A song by Sky Water began to play, a group with an ethereal sound: "If you love him, free him, if you love him, free him".

A voice inside her told her to take Pancake for a walk. She couldn't resist the urge. She knew she had to show some love to her beloved companion.

Maple put the leash on Pancake and took him to the same park she had visited earlier, Marina Willows. The walk with her faithful companion was a bonding experience, which calmed her racing thoughts and emotions.

However, as they walked through a part of the park that she affectionately referred to as "The Serengeti," an unexpected message echoed in her mind. It wasn't just a voice, it was a thought, strange and surreal.

"If you really love Pancake, set him free."

Maple was taken aback by the enigmatic message. It seemed to come out of nowhere, a riddle she couldn't decipher. But it resonated deep within her, and she realized it had a deep meaning.

With a broken heart, she unleashed Pancake, gave him a soft kiss, and whispered, "I will always love you. You are free."

Pancake, now unleashed, leaped like a frog, running through the grass and the rocky fields, and disappeared. Maple loved Pancake more than she loved herself. To her, Pancake was her number one, not just a dog, but a best friend, a confidant, a vessel of pure love, joy, and affection.

Alone in the park, Maple questioned the nature of her connection to Pancake. Overwhelmed by the moment, Maple put on her headphones and continued her walk, lost in a world of music and voices whispering in her head.

But then, something unusual began to happen. The music began to reveal hidden messages. The lyrics and melodies contained deeper meanings, which she had never noticed before. The lyrics described everything that surrounded Maple. "Beside the curling oaks, the crows stand free. Where the purple flowers rise, your footsteps will lead you. " She had heard these songs a million times, but they had never had such a deep meaning. Maple hesitated but walked toward the purple flowers with the pointed petals, beneath an oak tree with twisted branches where crows rested.

As Maple listened intently, she realized that something extraordinary was happening. The music itself tried to communicate with her, guiding her through a hidden path.

She rewound the song several times, each repetition bringing greater clarity to the message. It was as if the universe spoke to her through music, sharing its secrets and its wisdom. "He awaits. Hear the call. By the water, you'll be free..."

The message was clear: "Go to the ocean."

Following the guidance of music, Maple made it to the ocean. She kept walking, as if an invisible force were guiding her through the rocky terrain. Was this force the same force that had guided her to the mysterious berries? Maple wondered.

The song directed her to a specific place: "It's time to stop, you've arrived at the right place, this is where you need to be." Maple felt compelled to stop. She took a deep breath and took off her headphones, allowing the sound of the ocean to fill her ears.

As Maple stood on a rock, the vast expanse of the ocean stretched out infinitely before her. The skies were painted in shades of violet, tones that resonated deep within her soul. The sound of the furious waves crashing against the rocks made her body buzz like a bee. Maple's red locks danced in the wind like flames on a bonfire.

In the distance, hidden among the majestic mountains, an incredible sight captured Maple's attention. Maple wondered if her imagination was playing tricks on her. A colossal pair of eyes, reminiscent of those of a cat, seemed to stare at her with intensity. Those eyes shone with an otherworldly impetus, an enigmatic presence that sent shivers down her spine. The scene transcended the boundaries of the ordinary and entered the realm of the extraordinary. The gigantic eyes seemed to look directly into Maple's soul.

A multitude of symbols that seemed to be made of golden glitter landed in Maple's mind, each more mysterious than the last. They jumped in front of her like ancient alien hieroglyphs, telling a story that only she could comprehend.

Suddenly, she felt the colossal eyes communicate with her. Not through spoken words, but through a connection that transcended language. She could feel his presence, but not his intentions, a deep, intriguing voice that echoed within her very being.

The voice spoke to her, saying, "Maple, I am Mister Universe."

Maple was stunned, her heart racing with every second that seemed to be eternal. She couldn't believe what she was witnessing. This encounter with the colossal cat's eyes went beyond what she could have ever imagined. Maple believed in the possibility of the existence of a higher being, but she had always wondered if any of it was real. This was an unexpected revelation, one she wasn't prepared for.

The voice asked her a question, a question that pierced the depths of her soul: "Maple, what is your number one wish?"

Without hesitation, Maple replied, "I want the..." The voice completed Maple's thought: "... suffering in this world to end." Maple was in shock.

The voice then responded, "10:25."

He then posed another question: "What do you want for yourself, your deepest personal desire?"

Maple's thoughts racing when she saw an image in her mind. It was the image of a gray-haired man with a beautiful gray beard, and she saw a life of happiness and love unfolding before her eyes.

She was about to express her desire when Mister Universe said, "You want true eternal love."

In response, the cat-eyed entity revealed an image of the man once again, and Maple saw a future filled with fulfillment and happiness. She had no idea who this man was.

The colossal eyes of Mister Universe then gave her an ultimatum: "If you want everything you have ever dreamed of right now, jump into the ocean. If not, 10:25.

But remember, don't tell anyone what happened here today, because they'll think you've lost your mind.

Maple pondered the choice before her. The mysteries of Mister Universe had converged upon her, and the path she chose would define her destiny. The ocean was calling, but so was the enigmatic 10:25.

As Maple stood at the crossroads of reality and the unknown, she wondered what it all meant and what implications her decision would have.

However, she couldn't stop thinking about Pancake, which she had let run free in the park. With a heavy heart, she decided to leave the ocean behind for now and return to look for him. She didn't even say goodbye to Mister Universe. Maple felt a hint of sadness, torn between Mister Universe's offer and the eternal bond with her great weakness, her love, Pancake. She wanted that happy life for sure, but right now, Pancake needed her.

As she ran back home through the park, anxiety gnawed at her. Pancake was nowhere to be found. Panic set in and Maple began to cry inconsolably as she imagined the worst. She shouted his name as loudly as she could, repeatedly. Pancake was nowhere to be found. Suddenly, a voice in her head advised her to go home. Maple had to find Pancake, but the voice was really convincing.

Upon returning to the apartment, she discovered that she had lost the keys. She called Ria for help. Ria opened the door of the building remotely, her face a mixture of curiosity and concern.

Maple sounded distraught. Ria had no idea of the extraordinary adventure Maple had just embarked on.

When Maple finally arrived at her apartment, she was unexpectedly greeted by her sister, Honey, who was holding Pancake. Honey's eyes were filled with anger, and she couldn't contain her frustration. Ria decided to go to her bedroom.

"How could you leave Pancake alone like this?" Honey scolded Maple. "I was walking to the store, and I saw him running scared. I recognized him and ran three blocks behind him. Fortunately, I was able to grab him; He jumped on me and now my clothes are ruined, and I smell like a dirty dog." Honey berated Maple for her irresponsibility as a dog owner, and Maple could only offer an apology and a sincere "thank you."

Maple couldn't reveal the profound experiences she'd just gone through, the mysterious voice that had guided her, or the feline eyes that had communicated with her. The world she had entered was beyond comprehension.

She made up an excuse and apologized once again to Honey, who reluctantly accepted it and left Maple's apartment.

But the secrets she kept in her heart were too deep to be shared with anyone. When Honey left the apartment, Maple felt the need to create art, relieved that Pancake was safe.

Maple had always been a multifaceted artist, finding solace and expression through her creative daring. She had an eagerness to paint rocks, turning them into miniature masterpieces that she scattered throughout the city and around Marina Willows.

Years ago, she had created her own divination cards, a deck of seventy cards representing life, love, nature, the elements, stars, and even death. These cards had come to life through a mysterious inspiration. But tonight, Maple knew that a new card would be added to her deck, card 71: Mister Universe.

With determination and passion, she spent hours crafting the new card. In addition to the seventy-first card, she created another card without a name or number, a card that contained an enigmatic and strange figure. She didn't know where the inspiration came from; it was as if creativity flowed from the cosmos into her veins.

This unnamed card represented a woman with octopus-like limbs that served as her arms and legs. Her triangular-shaped head had two inverted horns, and a diamond adorned her forehead. She had a necklace made of rope and uneven, bare breasts. The figure rested on a cloud in front of a rainy background, with a rainbow shining below.

White flowers bloomed in the background, framing the mysterious woman.

Maple's handmade divination deck was now complete, and she had also improved her existing card designs. Little did she know that these cards would become her gateway to an unknown world.

When she placed the 71st card and the unnamed card in her deck, Maple felt a sense of anticipation and excitement. The adventure that awaited her was beyond her wildest dreams, a journey into the enigmatic realm of divination.

Chapter 3: Initiation

Maple felt a sense of excitement, her new divination cards resting on her bedside table. The enigmatic card she had created, the one that had no number, seemed to call her, its symbolism crying out to be understood. She wondered who or what the mysterious female figure represented.

As she held the cards, she couldn't shake the feeling that they held a magical secret, a hidden message waiting to be revealed. Maple had always been drawn to the mystical and the unknown, but this was something else entirely.

With a mixture of curiosity and apprehension, she decided to pull a card from her deck. The card she chose on purpose was the card she had just crafted, card number 71: Mister Universe. It was as if Mister Universe himself invited her to explore his mysteries. She closed her eyes, brought the card close to her heart, and whispered a question: "What do you have to reveal to me today, Mister Universe?"

After a deep breath, Maple turned the card over, and stared at its beautiful design for just a moment. It was beautifully illustrated, with galaxies, stars, and planets clattering together in a dance of creation. In the center of the card, there was the figure of the colossal cat eyes that contained the universe itself within.

Maple looked at the card, her mind open to any ideas or revelations that might come up. She felt a tingling sensation, as if a wave of energy was flooding her.

At that moment, she remembered the message of the cat's eyes by the ocean: "10:25." Could it be that this was the moment when Mister Universe would reveal his secrets to her? She looked at her watch; It was already 9:30. Time was running slowly.

Maple spent the next hour meditating and connecting with the card. She placed it on a small altar she had on a table in her apartment, surrounded by candles, sandalwood, semi-precious stones, shells, pieces of coral, and a small clay figure in the shape of a hunched old man sitting with bowed legs. When she closed her eyes, she entered a deep meditative state. She felt the undeniable energy of the card.

In this relaxed state of consciousness, she had visions of galaxies being born, stars exploding into bright supernovae, and the ebb and flow of cosmic energy. It was as if she had become part of the puzzle of the existence of everything. Somehow she could understand everything; All the impossible to decipher secrets were poured incessantly into her being.

As the minutes passed, she continued to receive symbols and messages, each one more intense than the last. She saw glimpses of ancient civilizations, Hidden art, and the interconnectedness of everything and everyone.

Maple suddenly felt a surge of energy. She felt a tingling sensation all over her body. She felt light as a feather. It was as if she was levitating.

Then she heard a voice, not from the card, but from her own mind. It was that unmistakable voice of Mister Universe, the mysterious entity with feline eyes that she had found by the sea.

"Maple," the voice echoed, "You have been chosen, your existence has a purpose beyond the ordinary. You are not a simple messenger; You have the absolute power to shape the world around you. You are a creator. Every action you take has great repercussions. Nothing is in vain; Every path you walk will be your guide. What you give to life, life will give back to you with immeasurable abundance. You are just being born," Mister Universe continued. "You will receive guidance and clues through the voices of wisdom and your divination cards. They have a special power. They are your keys to unlock the mysteries of your existence."

Maple listened intently. Her heart was beating with emotion. Mister Universe then spoke words that shook Maple to her core: "Magic is real."

Maple felt like a child full of illusions for this revelation from Mister Universe, she was being called to serve a higher purpose. She had always believed in the power of the universe, in its infinite wisdom and beauty, but now the allure of magic was revealed before her very eyes.

Mister Universe's voice echoed in her mind, "The road ahead is full of trials and questions, but you will never be alone again, even though you never really were. I will always be your constant companion and from now on I will guide you every step of the way." Always remember rule number one.

Then the voice fell silent.

With a sense of purpose bursting within her, Maple opened her eyes, feeling as if a new chapter of her life had just been released. Apparently, her divination cards were more than just tools for astrological understanding; they were a tangible connection to Mister Universe himself.

Maple couldn't stop thinking about the origin of her divination cards. She began to arrange the cards in front of her on the floor. Each card she carefully placed on the floor seemed to contain a unique message, a piece of the great puzzle of existence.

As she continued to place cards side by side and tried to decipher their meanings, Maple believed she had found a pattern. The cards seemed to be some kind of map, keys that were connected to known and unknown places and people. It was as if Mister Universe was whispering in her ear, using her divination cards as a magical conduit.

Maple remembered Mister Universe's warning not to reveal the true nature of her secret to anyone. She knew that the depth of her experiences was beyond most people's level of comprehension.

The next day, she woke up with an energy she had never felt before; she decided to text Honey, her direct supervisor and also her younger sister. The message read: "I quit; I'm heading for a walk through Marina Willows." She grabbed her divination deck and gave Pancake a big kiss before closing the door behind her. Her phone started ringing. The screen showed: Honey. Abruptly, she decided to leave her phone at home.

Maple went out, walked a few blocks, sat on a bench and took out a card: "The wall," Voices in her head began to give her directions. Maple listened to the voices and walked through different streets in circles until she found herself in front of a mural on a brick wall that had been painted with the images of orcas under the sea, apparently the mural had been done years ago, the art on the wall looked somewhat blurry, but strangely it seemed to come to life in front of Maple's incredulous eyes. The orcas seemed to swim freely, and Maple thought she heard their songs, and suddenly the symbols of the graffiti that had vandalized the mural moved and reorganized, forming a message that seemed to be as charged with magic as the experience she was living itself.

"The keys are hidden in plain sight," it said, before almost immediately returning to its original form.

The words of Mister Universe echoed in her head: Magic is real. She was confirming it with her own eyes.

Mister Universe was now her guide, and her divination cards were her direct connection to magic. Maple asked herself if what she was witnessing could be true. It all seemed to make sense. Maple now had a new purpose. She had to figure out what that purpose was, and apparently, all she had to do was keep her eyes very open and really pay attention to all the little details that she would normally let go unnoticed.

Chapter 4: Listen to the Voices

Maple suddenly found herself convinced that magic was real, and the most logical thing to do was to accept her role as a conduit for Mister Universe's messages. Her divination cards were no longer simple entertainment tools between glasses of wine and appletinis on girls' nights with Julie; Those crazy cards weren't so crazy now; they were her compass on a journey of discovery that defied logic and reason.

The hidden message in the vandal graffiti had become a new mission for Maple. "The clues are hidden in plain sight." This seemed to be a call that resonated deep within her soul.

With the cards in hand, Maple set out to explore the streets and interesting places in the city where she lived, Anacaona. Every place Maple walked through seemed to have a piece of the puzzle, hidden truths waiting to be discovered, and since Maple met Mister Universe, these secrets were being revealed to her with every step she took and, on top of that she had the unique opportunity to witness magic in the flesh, not in a fairy tale or in a video game, but with her own eyes, with the voices that communicated with her from the depths of herself.

Maple took a card from her deck, the card chosen at random "The Invisible Scroll", seemed to indicate that her next destination was the public library, a place that contained centuries of wisdom inside its walls. Maple headed towards Mount Jaragua Public Library and as she wandered through the maze-like hallways, a voice in her head told her that she had to find a specific book. The name Haja repeated itself like an echo in her head.

Suddenly Maple sees Ria, her roommate, who worked in the library. With a sense of anticipation, Maple approached her and greeted her affectionately with a hug. Ria felt a little uncomfortable. Ria was on the autism spectrum. Although she had gotten used to her job at the library, she always tried to keep interactions with other people to a minimum. But, she thought, it was only Maple after all, so she asked how she could help her. Maple said, "I need you to help me find a book. I don't know what it's called, but I know it contains the word Haja". Ria told Maple to follow her, and they went to the computer room, and Ria quickly but effectively taught her how to use the public computer to do searches. Maple opened the search page and typed: Haja. Maple saw the search results unfold on the screen, which seemed to speak to Maple. The computer had a strange energy. When she opened the only link that appeared on her screen, she did not find any books, but she found a passage that spoke of the interconnection of all things, of the threads that wove the mantle of the universe.

"The universe lives within you, you are the water that flows without ceasing, you are the fish that swims in all directions, you are the rock that treads the earth and the sea, you are the mineral that shines in the sunlight, you are the tree that stretches out to the sky and the flower that adorns the earth, you are the bird that flies freely, you are the air that fills the infinity of space, you are the sun, you are the moon, you are each and every star, you are every being that has ever lived or that ever will live, you are everything, and everything is you..."

Maple couldn't help but feel that Mister Universe himself was speaking to her through these words. It was as if he was revealing his secrets once again. Maple decided to look for Mister Universe's next clue, the most logical thing to do seemed to be drawing another card of hers.

Maple grabbed the deck and with two fingers she pulled out the card "The Forest of Contemplation". Her next destination couldn't be more obvious, it was clear that it was her favorite place, Marina Willows Park, a place she had visited countless times before, but now seemed to have a new meaning in her mission. "Maple, west is best," the voices in her head led her to Marina Willows, through the area Maple called the Serengeti toward Cuervo Hills, another one of Maple's nicknames for the many corners of Marina Willows.

On a rock at the top of Cuervo Hills, Maple took her shoes off her feet. She walked in some pain towards one oak tree in particular that stood proudly skyward, its twisted branches stretching in all directions. Perched on the branches were dozens of crows, which seemed to stare at Maple with great intensity.

When Maple touched the bark of the tree, all the crows began to screech at once. She felt a vibration of energy, a connection to the earth beneath her feet. As Maple looked up, she witnessed a beautiful rainbow. Then she whistled to the skies. As Maple's whistle echoed through the skies, the crows flew in unison. Earth itself seemed to have been sending her a message.

Maple decided to take another card from her deck, "The

Generous Garden, ", this was her next clue. Maple noticed that one of the crows in particular kept his eyes on her. Maple decides to follow him in flight. The crow flew small distances and stopped, giving Maple time to follow. Suddenly, the crow landed on a fruit basket at a market where they sold exotic fruits. Maple heard a voice telling her to talk to the vendor. The shapes, colors, and smells of the fruits seemed to radiate under a magical glow, but one fruit in particular caught her attention; A bunch of fruit that looked like small limes. Actually, she had no idea what this fruit was called, and she asked the vendor, who apparently had no idea what these round green fruits were called either.

The vendor was a skinny teenager who appeared to be the son of the shop owner; he had a name tag inscribed with the name Darwin on his shirt pocket. Out of nowhere, Darwin said that his grandmother had told him that those fruits held the secrets of love, the deepest and most enigmatic mystery of them all. Maple knew this was a message from Mister Universe, not just a wimpy teenager trying to make a sale, Maple knew she had to try that strange fruit, she asked the salesperson if she could try one, Darwin plucked one of the little green fruits and passed it to Maple. The shell was a bit soft but oddly tough on the outside. The most logical thing seemed to be to crack it open with her teeth, revealing a pinkish-orange pulp. Maple tasted the fruit in her mouth. It literally tasted like paradise. She then spat out a large whitish seed that she decided to place in her pocket.

The cards and voices continued to guide her through new and

unexpected destinies. Maple found herself walking through places she had never walked before. Each place seemed to have some sort of magic. With each place, she discovered one more piece of the puzzle, one more message that guided her to a deeper understanding of her own existence. Maple was beginning to see those threads that connected all things.

One night, as she sat on a bench in Marina Willows, staring at the stars, a sense of awe came over her. She could hear Mister Universe whispering in her head, "You are the chosen one." Finally, the magnitude of her experience became apparent in her head. She realized that Mister Universe was not just a distant and mysterious entity; He was a part of her, and she was a part of Him.

Maple decided to draw two cards from her divination deck at random, "The Infinite Pathway" and "The Society", when she was looking at the cards she felt a wave of happiness that flooded her, this had to be a message from Mister Universe himself. Maple had become a messenger of the secrets of the galaxy, and at that moment, she felt that the cards spoke to her.

As Maple wondered about the meaning of these cards, a voice whispered in her head, "You've been invited. Do you accept the invitation?"

Chapter 5: The Hidden Order

Maple had become obsessed with finding answers in the divination cards she had created. This quest had led her to numerous enigmatic places, each of which seemed to be just another piece of Mister Universe's puzzle. But as Maple accepted in the depths of her being that she was an important piece of this cosmic game, she also began to realize that everyone around her held enigmas that went beyond the ordinary. She understood that the heart of the city was not a bunch of concrete and steel buildings. The heart of the city was green, and it was blue. It was of all colors.

It was already a little late, Maple decided to draw a card from her deck, "The Lighthouse", suddenly a voice in her head told her to walk alone to Marina Willows, when she reached the edge of the park the voice told her to enter the park through a dimly lit access, where a single light projected long shadows on the grass. It was an access to the park that she had never ventured through before, much less at night. As she took her first steps down the winding path, the voice told Maple to take off her shoes. As she touched the grass with the soles of her feet, she felt as if she was walking in a totally different world. The magic was palpable at that moment.

As she curiously walked down a narrow path, Maple's senses intensified. An otherworldly energy could be felt in the air, and faint whispers could be heard in the darkness. It was as if the park itself was trying to communicate with her.

The voice in her head directed her towards some kind of portal, it was nothing ostentatious, nothing more than two wild berry bushes that formed an arc at the top. Maple hesitated for a moment, unsure of what she would find on the other side of this natural portal. But her sense of purpose and curiosity compelled her to step forward.

As she took a step further, Maple began to hear voices from other beings, who, like Maple, had been chosen to serve as Mister Universe's messengers. Without fully understanding it, Maple had entered a Hidden Order, a place that existed beyond the confines of time and space.

The beings chosen to be part of this order were diverse, beings from different walks of life, cultures and beliefs. They had all been called by Mister Universe to this hidden garden, to share their ancestral wisdom.

Maple heard voices welcoming her, she felt all the magic of the members of the Order within her being, who welcomed her with open arms and shared a wealth of knowledge with her. This portal seemed to be a place where the extraordinary was ordinary and Mister Universe's mysteries were alive.

In this Hidden Order, Maple discovered that the messages she received from her divination cards were not unique to her. Other beings were able to communicate with Mister Universe in a similar manner, and this select group of individuals had a transcendental purpose in the grandest plan of the existence of everything.

Maple received information from the voices of the Hidden Order who told her that Mister Universe's messages were not limited to her divination cards. The game's clues were woven into the very foundations of this world, hidden in plain sight for those who dared to discover them.

At the heart of Marina Willows, Maple and the members of the Hidden Order shared countless other enigmatic symbols, hidden truths, and ancient knowledge that had been passed down from generation to generation in past societies. It was a place where the ordinary became extraordinary and the mysteries of existence unraveled, here time seemed to vanish in the wind.

As the days turned into weeks, Maple continued to explore the Hidden Order, and with each passing second she deepened her understanding of the messages conveyed to her by Mister Universe. She realized that her journey on this earthly plane was not just about searching for answers, but about connecting with other beings who shared a grander purpose.

Together, members of the Order embarked on personal missions to unearth ancient secrets of humanity, deciphering symbols that had remained hidden for centuries. All the chosen beings could feel the enigmatic force that guided their lives from within, Mister Universe.

Maple's role as Mister Universe's messenger took on a new dimension within the Hidden Order. She was no longer alone in her search; she was now part of an elite, an elite chosen by Mister Universe himself to unravel the infinite mysteries of existence.

Each revelation received by the members of the Order connected them more closely Mister Universe, and united them all through a majestic force. The lucky ones knew that their purpose was not only to receive the messages from Mister Universe, but to share their wisdom with the world, so that more beings would open the eyes of the soul.

Maple understood with every spark of magic around her that her life had taken an unexpected turn, that the invitation to the Hidden Order had given her the keys to the mysterious locks of the world. Maple learned to receive the messages of Mister Universe without fear and as she continued to explore the secrets of life in Marina Willows' heart, Maple felt deep within herself that the magic she was witnessing was only beginning to unfold.

Chapter 6: In Search of the Island

Maple had become deeply intertwined with the Hidden Order, where she had learned more about Mister Universe's mysteries, even more than she could have ever imagined. Maple was sitting on her couch, Pancake lying on her lap, and as she shuffled her cards, she pulled out a new one: card number 31, the Overflowing Well. The card hid inside a beautiful illustration of a circular stone well, glistening with water gushing incessantly. Maple remembered creating this card, but honestly she had never really understood its meaning, or why she had created it.

When she least expected it, a voice who identified herself as "Cami" whispered in her head, "Haja Island has all the answers," but Maple had no knowledge of such a place. It was a name she had only heard once, when another voice in her head had spoken to her in the library, and apparently, this place actually existed, beyond the boundaries open to the public in Marina Willows Park. The search had now taken a new and unforeseen turn for Maple.

Maple was eager to discover the secrets that Haja Island had in store for her, so she decided to make contact with the Hidden Order, hoping to find guidance on finding the island. A voice that called himself "Ashraf" told her of a clue that could help her reach the island.

Ashraf's voice told her that this clue would be found deep in the Serengeti, in the area known as the "Cuervo Hills," under the tallest, curled oak tree. At that moment Maple felt illuminated by the light of the Hidden Order, Maple understood that there was no time to waste, she stood up from the sofa, filled Pancake with kisses and reminded him how much she loved him and embarked en route to Marina Willows to unearth the clue that would help her find her way to Haja Island.

Maple seemed to walk in circles through a maze of trails, long-forgotten passages deep within Marina Willows. Maple decided once again to take off her shoes and feel the energy of the earth on her feet. Each step brought her closer to her goal, and it was as if the park itself was guiding her path.

Maple was at the top of Cuervo Hills when suddenly, on the ground, something that shone like golden glitter captured Maple's attention. She felt at this moment that she had discovered some kind of ancient map; It wasn't just a map drawn on paper; it was a small gray speckled stone with some kind of alien symbols painted in a vivid golden color. Looking at the rock, Maple realized that she could connect the lines, dots and shapes inscribed on the small stone, the strange symbols seemed to tell a complex story, Maple's brain was able to decipher the symbols, this was undoubtedly a map of Marina Willows' immensity, she could see a path to the elusive island, the location of Haja Island was clearly visible, a place that existed beyond the public access area in the park, hidden in the middle of a blue lake.

With the magic rock in hand, Maple felt like her adventure was far from over. Haja Island apparently held secrets that were waiting to be discovered, and Maple was determined to get to it, and find Mister Universe's next clue.

Maple passed by the Duck Lagoon, and then passed through the yellow and white daffodil trails. She crossed under a wooden fence into Marina Willows Park. While heading to the lake, she saw a crow that seemed to follow her; she recognized him; it was not the first time she saw this crow; She noticed the distinctive markings on the rock, pointing westward. Maple whistled, and as the crow took flight, she decided to follow him on his flight. Maple suddenly found the blue lake, she marveled at the beauty of the crystal blue waters; the sun reflected like pure gold particles on the surface of the water. Maple couldn't believe what she was seeing. An island shone in the distance like a mirage. She had never seen that island before. Despite having been to the shores of that lake countless times, Maple used to jump over the wooden fences of the park.

Cami's voice shared her wisdom with Maple again, who felt a deep sense of belonging to the world around her. She felt like an important piece of a grand plan crafted by Mister Universe.

On the lake shore, there was no boat to be seen that could provide access to Haja Island, but there were rocks between the island and the shore. Maple decided she could swim to the island, stopping along the rocks that led to the island.

Maple took off her clothes and stayed in just her underwear, when she got into the water, the cold sensation on her skin injected her with an extraordinary dose of energy as she jumped into the water and began to swim, as if Mister Universe himself was pushing her forward, and best of all, she was not afraid at all. The shore was serene, and the lush, untamed beauty of the magic-filled island greeted her with vibrations that ran through her entire body. Maple's heart raced when she felt her feet touch the floor of the island, soaked from head to toe. The island was ridiculously beautiful; it was covered with all kinds of flowers of all colors, butterflies, bees, birds, and little mice. It was a place that seemed untouched by human hands.

Maple looked carefully at the markings on the rock inscribed in golden paint, with which she had swum and explored all the way to a path that seemed to call her by name, Cami's voice resounded in Maple's thoughts, she told her that she had to follow a parrot with white feathers on its forehead to a small hill where a perfectly round well made of stones of beautiful natural colors stood, in this majestic and perfect well, clear and pure waters gushed out without stopping. Upon seeing it, Maple gasped and realized that it had to be the same Overflowing Well from her divination deck.

Cami's voice spoke to her once more, urging her to take some water from the well and drink from it. Maple placed her hands like a cup and filled them with water that seemed to glow magically, when she took just one sip she felt an inexplicable surge of energy and ancestral knowledge, as if the majestic power of Mister Universe himself flowed through her veins, it not only tasted of water, it tasted of the most delicious flavors of the world, when Maple closed her eyes, she could taste true happiness.

Maple felt soaked in knowledge and fulfillment for a brief moment, Maple contemplated the stunning scenery of the island and understood that every moment in her life had brought her to this place for some unknown reason. Haja Island held secrets waiting to be investigated, and Maple was ready to fully immerse herself in Mister Universe's game and be filled with his wisdom from beyond.

As she stood by the edge of the Overflowing Well, the voice of Mister Universe himself echoed in her mind: "Maple, your quest is not only about seeking answers to all your curiosities about existence, but about becoming a guardian of the world around you, you have the power to drown the suffering of many in your passage through this life, this opportunity that you will only experience once, in eternity, well, this specific life, because they are infinite lives and different ways of living them, with different challenges... You understand..."

Maple absorbed Mister Universe's revelations deep within her soul and decided to leave the island and head on her way to the Hidden Order of Marina Willows, entering through the labyrinth that led to the magical portal that held the wisdom of the ones chosen by Mister Universe, she shared her experience with the other Illuminated beings. The beings revealed to her that they too had embarked on their own adventures in Mister Universe's grand game, revealing visions of their unique experiences and perceptions to her.

For Maple, the search for Haja Island had opened Pandora's box, and she could feel within her being that the magic on her path was far from over. Her connection to Mister Universe seemed to grow stronger with every breath.

Chapter 7: The Offering

Mister Universe's messages had led Maple to Haja Island again, and as she walked towards the Overflowing Well, she heard Cami's voice back in her head. "Haja Island asks you for an offering, the greatest offering that your heart allows, if you wish to know the secrets of existence and accept the call from Mister Universe; you must bring more life to the island. Mother Haja will reveal the way to true happiness."

Maple was puzzled. Haja Island was already lush and prosperous, teeming with life. It was as if nature had created a sanctuary of its own in this hidden gem. But the voices communicating with Maple were persistent and compelling, and Maple felt a deep connection to her guides.

Every day Maple returned to the island, bringing with her the offerings that the voices had asked for. She would kneel by the well and talk to Mister Universe, then with the water from the well she would begin to sprinkle the soil, plant wildflower seeds she bought online, and spend hours carefully observing the new flowers she found on each of her trips to the island. She would scatter seeds for the birds to eat and they would spread it even more all over the island, this seemed to be an invitation for little creatures of all colors, sizes and shapes to feast and contribute to the majestic plan that Maple could not fully comprehend, despite all the magic she was immersed in these days.

As days turned into weeks, Maple noticed something truly amazing happening on Haja Island. The already lush landscape began to transform even more, as if the island was waking up from a long slumber. Fresh flowers of vibrant colors bloomed, and the trees grew taller and stronger. Birds with feathers of all colors flocked to the island, their songs filled the air with magic.

The island came alive with dazzling vitality, and Maple realized that her offerings were not just gifts to an island, but opened a direct line that connected her to the awesome power of Mister Universe himself, in the form of happiness and purpose. It was as if she had become a guardian of this sacred place, a protector of the life that flourished before her eyes and her actions.

The voices of wisdom whispered to her that Mister Universe was able to show her the true power that lay in her hands, the power of improving the world around her. It was a lesson that transcended the boundaries of the island and beyond.

With more understanding within her being, Maple continued to visit Haja Island, each day bringing more offerings of soil, flower seeds, plants, and food for the island's birds and small creatures. She also brought with her stones that she herself painstakingly painted with beautiful designs inspired by the majesty of nature, on nights when her mind was very active. The island had become a place of deep connection, a place where she communicated with the heart of nature and with Mister Universe, of course.

Maple, of course, shared her experiences with the Hidden Order, and other beings of light were inspired to be agents of the majestic change that was slowly cooking. In various corners of the world, parks and green spaces began to bloom with new vitality. More and more people were feeling the magic present on Haja Island.

The search for Haja Island had not only revealed countless secrets to her, but it had also revealed deeper clues about Maple's purpose as Mister Universe's messenger. She wasn't just a recipient of his messages; She was a commissioner, a caretaker, a guardian of nature.

The journey in search of a grander purpose within Maple continued, and one summer day, as she stood by the Overflowing Well on Haja Island, she drank from its crystal-clear water that ran non-stop and felt a buzz throughout her whole body, a deep connection with Mister Universe, she knew that he, the super-powerful Mister Universe had a purpose for her, Maple... And this purpose was becoming clearer every day. Maple felt boundless, indescribable happiness as she accepted the keys to her true calling.

Chapter 8: Return to Haja Island

Maple awoke from her slumber, the vivid memories of her time on Haja Island still fresh in her mind. She couldn't shake the feeling that her experiences on the island were more than a dream; They felt like a deep, tangible reality.

Unable to refuse Mister Universe's call, she decided to embark on one more journey to Haja Island. She was determined to prove that the island in the lake really existed, or if it had been just a very convincing creation of her own imagination.

With her divination deck in her hands and the echoes of the island's beauty in her heart, Maple made her way to the place that the stone with golden symbols had taken her in her dreams. Maple's heart was filled with anticipation and uncertainty. The voices of wisdom guided her with every step she took.

When she reached the shores of the blue lake, she was relieved to see Haja Island shining in the distance. It was not a mirage, and it was a proof of her connection to Mister Universe and to her own reality.

She swam to the island once more, realizing that it was as beautiful and full of life as she remembered. The flowers on the ground, the leafy trees, and the sounds of birds were there, just as they had been in her dream.

Maple approached the Overflowing Well, the very well of her dream. It was real, and its waters flowed incessantly. It was obvious that her connection to Mister Universe was not limited to her dreams.

The island, it seemed, was a bridge between the realms of dreams and reality, a place where the messages of Mister Universe could be felt in the flesh. Maple wasn't just a messenger; She was also a bridge between worlds.

Realizing that her experiences on Haja Island were not a simple dream, but a profound reality, Maple returned to the Hidden Order to pass on her knowledge to the other beings of light.

The island was a sacred place for the beings of the Hidden Order, a place where the power of Mister Universe flowed freely. Haja Island was proof that the boundaries between dreams and reality were often more fluid than one might expect.

While Maple continued to soak in revelations, with Haja Island as a tangible connection to all the power of Mister Universe.

Haja Island was a sanctuary, and the light beings of the Hidden Order were recipients of the boundless wisdom of the cosmos.

Maple suddenly opened her eyes.

Chapter 9: Cuervo Hills

When Maple opened her eyes again, she couldn't shake the feeling that she was experiencing a series of interconnected dreams, a web of incidents that blurred the lines between reality and fantasy. Cami's voice called her to Cuervo Hills, a part of Marina Willows Park where crows were known to congregate. "Mister Universe has summoned you, Maple, don't keep him waiting."

Maple heeded Cami's call and headed to Cuervo Hills with a bag full of leftover food in her hand to feed the crows. Maple whistled with a particular rhythm; The crows, with their dark, knowing eyes, clustered around her. Maple was standing on a large rock at the top of the small hill, turned toward the sun, and opened her eyes for a split second. Suddenly, a strange symbol was imprinted in her mind. It resembled the golden alien symbols of the stone that had led her to Haja Island.

With the symbol etched into her consciousness, Maple searched within herself for the voice she had conversed with multiple times on Haja Island by the Overflowing Well, none other than the enigmatic Mister Universe. Maple needed urgent answers to the questions that had plagued her since the explosion of magic in her life.

Standing among the crows in Cuervo Hills, Maple spoke aloud to Mister Universe, asking for guidance and understanding. The symbol in her mind began to take shape and, with a beat of her heart, she felt his presence.

The deep and intriguing voice of Mister Universe filled her thoughts, and he began to unravel the mysteries of her dreams; "Maple, Haja Island, and the Hidden Order are not just simple dreams, they are actually portals to a deeper understanding of existence."

Mister Universe explained that He communicated with chosen individuals in ways that transcended the limits of the ordinary. Dreams were just one of those ways, a realm where his messages could be received and deciphered by those with their eyes wide open.

He further explained that the dreams of Haja Island had been an invitation, an initiation into a Hidden Order of beings of light who shared a deep connection with him, Mister Universe himself. With these words, Maple understood that she was not alone in her search, but that she was part of something much grander and much more majestic.

The mysterious symbols and strange messages were the language of the galaxy, a way for Mister Universe to communicate truths and unearth mysteries to those who were willing to listen closely. Those symbols, like the one she experienced in Cuervo Hills, held the key to opening up a greater understanding of her existence.

Maple was no longer trapped in a series of dreams; she was a traveler of the cosmos, a real messenger of Mister Universe, and a guardian of the sacred knowledge that connected the Hidden Order, Haja Island, and all the enigmatic symbols that Maple encountered in her path, which were made with intention and purpose.

Mister Universe was her guide, Marina Willows was her

sanctuary, and the Hidden Order was her connection to a network full of magic.

Chapter 10: The Painted Rock

At the top of Cuervo Hills, as Maple stood next to a large oak tree with twisted branches, absorbing the revelations of Mister Universe, something peculiar by her feet caught her attention. It was a painted rock, much like the ones she used to paint, very similar to that image of the numberless card in her divination deck. Strangely enough, she didn't remember painting this beautiful rock, but it certainly eerily reminded her of her own creations.

Astonished by the coincidence, she picked up the rock and turned it over. There, on the back, were written the words: "Find yourself in Haja Island." Inscribed in radiant gold paint. The rock felt again like a tangible link between her dreams and her reality, like a bridge that connected fantasy with reality. Magic seemed to be in fact real.

Maple realized that Mister Universe was calling her to Haja Island, not only in her dreams but also in her awakening. The meticulously painted rock was certainly more than just an invitation. It was a reminder that the mysteries of the island were not limited to her dreams but were woven into the veil of her existence.

The Hidden Order had taught her valuable lessons about nurturing the world around her, about giving back to nature. Now, it seemed, Mister Universe was calling her again to embark on a journey of self-discovery, to "find herself" in the fantastic world of Haja Island.

Maple grabbed the painted rock in her hand, and when she felt its cold surface, she knew that her path was already traced. She would return to Haja Island again, not as a mere dreamer, but as a woman with a real purpose in this life. Maple was sure that the island held secrets that were waiting to be discovered, not just secrets about the mysterious, majestic game of Mister Universe, but about herself.

Maple had a new purpose; to explore the depths of her own existence.

Maple's journey of self-discovery was just beginning, and that painted rock was a tangible symbol of the wisdom of the cosmos. Cuervo Hills was just a starting point.

Chapter 11: The Blue Lake

Maple was standing under a majestic oak tree with twisted branches in the middle of Cuervo Hills with that painstakingly painted rock in her hands. Suddenly, she came to a daunting realization. There was no Hidden Order, no magical beings to accompany her in her search for the truths of existence. The revelations, the dreams, and everything she had experienced deep within her being, were experiences she had to face alone.

However, for Maple, the determination to find Haja Island remained unwavering. She knew that this time she had to walk on her own. Mister Universe had already guided her to the moment she was in, and that painted rock was surely an invitation, and now Maple would embark on the journey towards the truth as a solo traveler.

Maple couldn't stop thinking about that strange symbol imprinted in her mind as she stared at the sun during her visit to Cuervo Hills. Now Maple only had her own intuition and the experiences full of pure magic that she had lived in the flesh. This symbol had to be a clue.

With the symbol etched in her mind, she began exploring beyond the boundaries of Marina Willows Park. Maple became so obsessed that she studied maps at the library, consulted the Internet, and looked up information about hidden lakes and islands. Maple knew that Haja Island existed in the real world, just as it existed in her dreams.

Days turned into weeks, and Maple's determination only grew stronger. Visiting the park every day, exploring every corner, often interacting with the crows in Cuervo Hills, and following any clues that might lead her to the island, Maple sensed that the symbol would be the one that would show her the way.

While searching for clues on the internet, she stumbled upon a reference to a small island in the center of a lake outside the public boundaries of Willows Marine Park, to the west, known only to a few. The description matched her dreams of Haja Island. Seen from space, the island had a shape similar to that symbol imprinted on her head when she looked directly at the sun in Cuervo Hills.

Maple's heart raced with excitement. She had finally found a concrete clue, a way to make her dreams come true. Maple filled her backpack with everything she needed for her journey to Haja Island.

The journey was not without its challenges, and Maple faced physical and emotional obstacles along the way. But she was determined to prove to herself that she wasn't crazy, driven by the connection she'd forged with Mister Universe. To get to the island, she would have to swim long distances, but just like in her dream, there were rocks where she could stop and recover.

Maple had walked west and found that blue lake that refused to be discovered. Swimming towards the shores of the island that could be seen in the distance, soaked from head to toe, she arrived at Haja Island, that place where dreams, reality, and unlimited mysteries converged, to discover its secrets, and, most importantly, to find herself.

Chapter 12: The Deserted Island

The excitement on Maple's face was palpable as she got closer to the abandoned island she believed to be Haja Island. Mister Universe had guided her to this place, and she was determined to uncover its mysteries.

However, as soon as she set foot on the island, she noticed something peculiar. Unlike the lush and vibrant Haja Island of her dreams, this island was barren. There was no sign of flowers sprouting in the pastures, no leafy trees or birds singing. The landscape was a desolate one, and the sense of vitality, which had previously been overwhelming, was replaced by an eerie silence.

Maple was walking through the desolate landscape, when she suddenly noticed a circular rock formation much like the Overflowing Well of her dreams. But instead of emanating water, this well was dry, dusty, as if it had never known the coolness of water. The stark contrast to that well full of life and abundance in her dreams was overwhelming.

Maple continued to explore the island, and the barrenness became more apparent. There were no signs of the Hidden Order, no beings of light, and no Mister Universe. Maple found herself alone on this barren island, facing a harsh reality that seemed to negate the dreams that had brought her here.

Confusion and doubt began to invade her mind. Had she made a mistake? Had Mister Universe played a mean joke on her? Maple couldn't help but question the validity of her experiences.

However, she couldn't ignore the beautifully decorated rock she held in her hands. She couldn't deny that symbol imprinted on her mind and the vivid dreams that had guided her there. There had to be a reason for this seemingly lifeless island, a lesson or a revelation that she needed to discover.

The well was her starting point. Maple was determined to explore every inch of the island, looking for Mister Universe's clues. He had been her guide until now, and she refused to forget all the magic she had been exposed to.

As Maple wandered aimlessly around the island, contemplating the connection between the lush landscapes of Haja Island in her dreams and the harsh reality of this dry, dusty place, she found herself wandering through. Mister Universe had chosen her for a reason, and she knew that she had to find out what that reason was. Maple then took the seed she had in her pocket, the mysterious fruit from the exotic fruit market, and threw it into the bottom of the well and waited for something to happen, but nothing happened.

Chapter 13: Rebirth

Determined to transform the dusty island into a lush paradise like the one she had imagined in her dreams, Maple embarked on a daily pilgrimage. Before leaving home and saying goodbye to her beloved Pancake, she would fill her backpack with bags of soil, seeds, small plants she found on the streets, and head back to that desolate island, carrying with her a different card from her divination deck each day.

Each of the cards carried its own symbolism and message, and Maple saw them as her guidelines for what to plant and what to bring to the island. Mister Universe, it seemed, was still guiding her, though in a different way than her dreams had suggested.

With unwavering determination, Maple began her work. Each day, she planted new life on the island, seeking to bring the abundance and vitality she had seen in vivid colors in her dreams. It was a labor of love and a reflection of her deep connection to Mister Universe.

Days turned into weeks, and then months, and Haja Island was beginning to be reborn. The seeds that Maple had scattered, with the help of the birds that ate them, had sprouted everywhere, the plants had begun to produce roots, and the small tree cuttings had begun to grow. Gradually, the landscape began to teem with life, as if Mister Universe was responding to Maple's every effort.

Maple had not only found Haja Island; but was also in the process of co-creating it, in the shadows of Mister Universe. These small and large changes on the island were living proof of Maple's connection to the cosmos, a reminder that her dreams, her visions, and most of all, her actions could shape reality.

The well, which was once completely dry, began to show signs of water. That barren island was slowly becoming a pure symbol of life. It was undoubtedly majestic, that creative power of Mister Universe, the magic of nature and the determination of a woman full of inner light.

Maple's Pilgrimage was not just about transforming the island; It was about finding herself in the process. Maple had discovered that her connection to Mister Universe wasn't limited to her dreams, but that she could make the world around her a better place with just a small action.

That beautifully painted rock, which had been more than just an invitation, now had an even deeper meaning. It was a symbol of her journey; it was a physical reminder that Mister Universe required action and commitment on her part if she really wanted to see her vision of Haja Island become a reality and, in the process, find herself in the midst of that place so full of magic.

Chapter 14: Mother Haja

As Maple's daily pilgrimage to the not-so-barren island continued, she took off her shoes and connected more deeply with the land and with those symbols that had guided her there. One day, as she stood in front of the thriving garden that had grown from her creation, she looked carefully at that rock minutely painted with the image of that strange female figure on that numberless card. This rock had become a source of inspiration and an important symbol of her magical adventure.

Out of nowhere, in a moment of profound enlightenment, Maple decided to name this unique and mysterious card "Mother Haja." It seemed to be an appropriate name for the card that had helped her reach the island and that was now guiding her on her mission to restore its beauty and strength.

As she named that card, Maple's deep connection to the island was even more palpable, as if it were a living entity in itself, a mother who had nurtured her dreams. Maple was now witnessing that transformation in real life.

The name "Mother Haja" for some reason had a deep meaning for Maple, it was like a symbol of the power of dreams, and it was also a tribute to all mothers, especially to her own mother, Pearl, her guide in many ways throughout her life long before she met Mister Universe and understood her own potential as an agent of transformation.

Mother Haja's mystical presence on the island felt more and more persistent with each passing day, as if that enigmatic figure depicted in that card had become a living being watching over Maple's efforts. This island was undoubtedly a source of inspiration, but it was also her way of processing all the power that lay in her connection with Mister Universe.

Maple felt an indescribable gratitude to Mother Haja, and also to that majestically decorated rock that had helped her on this transformative journey. That rock was a tangible symbol of her own growth, of her ability to create a profound impact inspired by her dreams and her reality.

The truth is that Maple continued to make her daily pilgrimage to Haja Island, nurturing the land and the life that was slowly returning to that once-barren island, and her connection to Mister Universe was a source of strength and guidance in this adventure that seemed far from over.

The work to restore the island gave Maple deep satisfaction. Having found Haja Island, not only in her dreams, but in reality, strengthened her relationship with Mister Universe.

Mother Haja had also become her guide, and that lush garden was more than evidence of her efforts. Maple had begun to decipher the limitless mysteries of existence and to share all that wisdom she had acquired with the enlightened voices that made contact with her.

Chapter 15: Unanswered Questions

Maple's usual pilgrimage to Haja Island showed no signs of stopping. Maple was captivated and even haunted by the magic of the island teeming with exuberant and vibrant life, that pure magic she had worked so hard to cultivate. The aridity of the island had finally been transformed into a ridiculously beautiful and prosperous garden.

However, there was one aspect of that adventure that Maple continued to live that remained shrouded in utter mystery: that enigmatic message she had received during her first encounter with Mister Universe, "10:25." Despite all her efforts and the transformation of the island, this message remained unexplained.

Maple often found herself pondering the real and profound meaning of 10:25. It was a cryptic code, a time, a date, or perhaps something else entirely. Mister Universe had uttered it among his many revelations that day, and Maple couldn't help but feel that the mysterious 10:25 was an important key to her overall purpose in life. The truth is, even though Maple had received a message from Mister Universe himself at exactly 10:25 after meeting him in the ocean, she still couldn't get a doubt out of her head... Why 10:25?

At this moment the most logical thing seemed to be to use the power of her cards, meditate and even ask Mister Universe for guidance, but no matter how hard she tried to decipher the meaning of 10:25, it remained unattainable. It was as if Mister Universe was giving her a puzzle, an enigma that required her to delve deeper into the reality of her own existence and the world around her.

While the lush beauty of Haja Island and its connection to Mother Haja were profound and transformative, the unanswered question of 10:25 kept haunting Maple's mind, Mister Universe's games were not always straightforward. There were depths to which Maple was not yet able to dive in, no matter how much magic she had at her disposal at that moment.

Maple, for some reason, was able to understand that her adventure was not over yet, and that the mysteries that had brought her to this point were an invitation to continue exploring and co-creating with the help of Mister Universe, who had guided her to this moment, and she was ready to welcome the limitless possibilities that lay ahead with open arms.

Chapter 16: Seeking Help

Julie had been a confidante and an unwavering source of support for Maple for most of her life. Maple decided to call her. When the phone rang, Julie answered friendly. After greeting her and asking her how she, Sam and their cat Bagel were, Maple told her that she had been experiencing some incredible things and that she wanted to share with her each of the details of her latest experiences, and began to talk, like an open faucet, she began to tell her about the profound transformation of Haja Island, she told her about Mother Haja's love and about the lingering mystery of "10:25", Julie let her speak, listening attentively without interrupting her. Maple vented to her best friend as she had done a thousand times before.

After listening carefully to the incredible, but not so believable, adventures that Maple joyfully told her about, Julie could only think deeply about how to help her dearest friend. She knew that Maple wasn't crazy and that the experiences she'd had were far from ordinary. Julie was the daughter of a psychologist, after all, and she understood mental health disorders a little bit. In her quest to understand Mister Universe and herself, Maple had embarked on a unique journey deep into the confines of her mind. Julie understood that she had to be subtle in her ways of helping her best friend.

Julie had an idea that might offer Maple some perspective. She suggested that Maple visit her mother, Dinorah, who was a therapist and psychologist. Without a doubt Dinorah had a very particular style, therapies that implied the use of puppets as a means of understanding and self-discovery.

Dinorah's innovative, but unusual therapeutic methods had supposedly helped hundreds of people find clarity, cope with challenges, and navigate the complexities of life. Julie believed that Dinorah's experience could provide Maple with a new perspective on her life and purpose. Perhaps, if Maple learned to manage her emotions, she could live a normal life.

Maple listened to her friend Julie's worried but optimistic words and considered the idea. After thinking about it a little more, she thought it wouldn't hurt to seek guidance from a professional who specialized in helping people like her explore their inner worlds. She decided to contact Dinorah and schedule a session with her.

On the day of the therapy session with Julie's mother, Dinorah Goldbucket, Maple couldn't help but feel a strange mixture of excitement and apprehension. She had already opened her heart to the teachings of Mister Universe, and now she was opening her mind to the possibility of understanding the profound experiences that had shaped her existence.

The energy of Mother Haja and her lush garden, the inexhaustible wisdom of Mister Universe, and the lingering mystery of "10:25" were at the forefront of Maple's thoughts, but she was prepared to embrace the therapy session and see where it could take her.

Chapter 17: Dr. Goldbucket

Maple's long-awaited appointment with Dr. Dinorah Goldbucket promised to be an escape route from the intensity of all her experiences, a chance to vent about those utterly magical and extraordinary events that had become the essence of her life. However, when she settled into the cozy emerald green couch, everything took an unexpected turn.

Dr. Goldbucket had a confrontational therapy style. The therapist, known for her unorthodox methods with the use of puppets, gave Maple the space and time to feel comfortable, recounting her experiences from the day she stumbled upon the elusive white berry.

Maple went out of her way to tell her story, narrating her encounters with Mister Universe, the mysterious Haja Island, the Hidden Order, and the peculiar clues scattered throughout Marina Willows. As Maple spoke, a puppet resembling Maple herself, with fiery red hair and piercing blue eyes, seemed to absorb absolutely every detail. It seemed as if the puppet was not just a passive observer, but rather, an active participant, causing Maple to squeeze out even the smallest details of her interactions with Mister Universe and all the magic-filled events that were connected.

Dr. Dinorah Goldbucket was also deeply engrossed in Maple's storytelling, paying meticulous attention to each word and taking notes in her notebook. However, despite offering empathy, she did not give Maple the validation of her magical experiences as she had hoped.

Dinorah opted for a different approach, unhesitatingly questioning Maple's belief in the magical elements woven into her story, totally challenging the perception of what was reality in Maple. In the middle of the session, Dinorah coolly suggested that Maple might benefit most from the expertise of a psychiatrist with expertise in bipolar disorders.

Maple, who initially hoped to find understanding and support, felt a wave of frustration and confusion wash over her. The session had not been as she had imagined it would be; she went through it thousands of times in her head, leaving her in a state of shock, questioning not only the validity of her experiences but also the direction her journey had taken in search of truth and purpose. As the puppet continued to talk, and Dr. Goldbucket dug deeper, Maple grappled with the idea that the sanctuary of understanding she sought in the session had become a battleground filled with skepticism and doubt. The elusive white berry in the shape of a tiny velvety peach that had once been a source of magic and enlightenment now seemed to symbolize the uncertainty that clouded Maple's quest for an understanding of her existence.

After the appointment, already at home, feeling very restless, Maple decided to take a walk through Marina Willows, the place where her adventure full of magic had begun. She needed to clear her mind and reflect on the most recent events. Mister Universe had guided her through amazing experiences, but now Maple was facing the uncertainty of having to seek professional help for what could be a mental illness.

As Maple walked through the park with her headphones blaring listening to the music of Sky Water, the memories of her trips to Haja Island and the transformation of that barren landscape into a thriving garden full of life and exuberance filled her thoughts. Maple couldn't help but wonder if her experiences were completely real, unique, and meaningful or if they were, as Dinorah had suggested, a sign of something more serious.

Julie's words echoed in her mind: "I don't know, but maybe seeing a psychiatrist might be a good idea." Maple's frustration and uncertainty continued to bubble up deep within her being. Maple had always believed in the power of dreams and the magic of the universe, but now she was at a crossroads.

While a part of her wanted to rely on memories of her own experiences and intuition about what's real and what's not, another part of her being simply couldn't ignore the concerns raised by both Dinorah and, her best friend Julie. The great mystery of "10:25" and the depths of her connection to Mister Universe weighed heavily on her mind.

Maple walked through Marina Willows, trying to calm her anxiety, enjoying the spectacular beauty and serenity that the park had always known how to offer her. All the majesty that once upon a time had inspired her, was still there, as a reminder of the magic that had brought her to Haja Island.

The next steps in her mission were unclear. She had a choice to make. Continue to discover all the magic that Mister Universe had to give her, seek guidance from a psychiatrist, or simply try to find some way to bridge the gap between her extraordinary experiences and the concerns of those around her.

Every step Maple took in Marina Willows, made her reflect on the labyrinth that lay ahead, not knowing where it could lead her.

Chapter 18: The Majestic Peacock

In the middle of her contemplative walk through Marina Willows, Maple reached into her pocket and pulled out her deck of divination cards. Looking for some clarity and guidance, she decided to draw a card, and, to her surprise, it was one of her favorite cards, number 13: The Majestic Peacock.

The image of the peacock meticulously illustrated in the card that Maple had created with her divine inspiration was a vivid display of vibrant feathers, and a royal presence. Maple couldn't help but be impressed by the symbolism of the card and the message it brought with it.

The Majestic Peacock was a symbol of beauty, confidence, and self-expression. In nature, the male peacock was a creature known for the dazzling display of its vibrant plumage when courting a peahen. The dance it performed managed to capture the attention of all who contemplated it. The peacock was considered a symbol of great importance in many ancient cultures, often representing renewal, transformation, and rebirth.

Maple looked at the card and couldn't help but wonder about its message. What was Mister Universe trying to tell her through the Majestic Peacock?

The peacock's beauty and confidence were qualities that Maple had also discovered within herself during her romance with magic.

She had been able to transform a barren island into an exuberant garden, and she had done so by letting herself be guided by her dreams and trying to reveal Mister Universe's mysteries. Her whole adventure was in itself a display of self-expression, renewal, and transformation, and Maple possessed the strength and inner beauty to face the uncertainties that remained in her head.

With the card in hand, Maple contemplated her next steps. The message conveyed by the card invited her to accept her own beauty and uniqueness, just as the peacock flaunted his magnificent plumage.

As she continued her walk through Marina Willows, the symbolism of the Majestic Peacock did not escape her thoughts, and Maple felt a renewed sense of determination deep within her.

Suddenly, something extraordinary began to happen. Voices in her head led her to find eight peacock feathers scattered throughout the park.

Each of these feathers had a distinct meaning, and as Maple found them, she couldn't help but feel a sense of validation. The beautiful peacock feathers were tangible symbols that provided evidence of her unique connection to Mister Universe, a connection that had led her to visit Haja Island.

Maple held eight peacock feathers in her hands, and her purpose and determination were renewed. These feathers were also concrete proof that her experiences were not signs of madness, but rather evidence of her deep connection with Mister Universe.

With feathers as her companions, Maple continued her journey of self-discovery and desired nothing more than to share the wisdom she had gained with the world. The enigma of "10:25" was waiting to be deciphered, and perhaps these feathers were one more clue.

As she made her way through Marina Willows, Maple couldn't help but reflect on the guidance she had received from the voices in her head. These voices had led her to finding the peacock feathers, providing her with a sense of validation in her experiences. However, the lingering mystery of "10:25" was what weighed most heavily on her mind.

Maple knew that Mister Universe had unique ways of communicating with her, and perhaps the peacock feathers were a sign of that. With them in hand, she felt a deeper connection to the beauty and complexity of life, a connection that transcended the ordinary and reminded her of the beauty that existed deep within her being.

In her mind she also considered the symbolism of feathers as signs of grace, balance, and creativity, thus understanding that all the magic she had experienced was only a delicate dance with Mister Universe. Intuition and introspection were qualities she had developed throughout her dance with Mister Universe, and the feathers Maple had found only affirmed their importance.

Unanswered questions and unexplored depths still tormented her. Suddenly, on her way home, as she passed through the Serengeti, she saw a majestic peacock that only reinforced the message of self-expression and beauty that pulsated within Maple, echoing that card she had chosen at random.

Maple decided to keep the peacock feathers as a constant reminder of her intimate relationship with Mister Universe and as a validation of her experiences on that unique and special path, she knew that sooner or later she would be able to decipher those clues that could help her discover the meaning behind the "10:25". That mystery of her awakening was still unfolding.

Chapter 19: Seeking Professional Help

Maple had always known that her sister, Honey, was a down-to-earth woman, with her dry and above all level-headed personality. In her naïve mind, she believed that telling Honey about her extraordinary experiences and about those voices that were communicating with her in her head would make her understand, and perhaps join her in her mission to make the world a better place. Maple finally decided to trust Honey and prepared for her reaction.

Maple began to excitedly tell her about the whole adventure, she talked about the velvety white berries, her connection with Haja Island, she told her about the peacock feathers and especially the mysterious "10:25", Honey listened attentively, but her face showed a strange mixture of disbelief, amazement and concern. Maple finally finished speaking. Honey, didn't waste a second and was quick to express her doubts, suggesting almost instantly that Maple might be experiencing delusions or a form of psychosis.

Unlike her mother, Pearl, who was a gentle soul with a deep connection to the spiritual and mystical, Honey had always opted for a more direct, practical, and grounded approach to life. Honey's almost immediate response was to call a psychiatrist and schedule an appointment for Maple.

Although Honey didn't like to show signs of emotion or concern, the truth is that she was scared, and her uneasiness about her sister's well-being was evident, but for Maple, this was like a slap in the face.

She couldn't help but feel frustrated and misunderstood. How could it be that Honey wasn't able to understand rule number one? Maple had hoped that her experiences would be greeted with perhaps little skepticism, but it was certainly disheartening to hear her own sister question her sanity.

Reluctantly, Maple agreed to visit the psychiatrist. Maple knew she needed to explore every avenue to understand the voices she kept hearing in her head: Cami, Ashraf, Orlando, Elba, Angelica, Fenil, Nilda, Melissa and all the others. These voices were undoubtedly convincing. In addition, Maple wanted to understand all the mysteries that had guided her extraordinary adventure. A psychiatrist could perhaps offer her a different perspective, one that could help her make sense of her amazing experiences.

As the day of her appointment with Dr. Woodfire approached, Maple couldn't help but feel a mixture of fear and excitement. She was open to the possibility that it was probable that the psychiatrist could provide her with valuable information that would help her in the search for her purpose in life, but more than anything she hoped to find some way to bridge the gap between her desire to continue living in the midst of magic and the worries of those around her.

The voices in her head had become her constant companions, and Maple had decorated her apartment with the peacock feathers she had found as a souvenir of her connection to Mister Universe, Maple felt ready to embark on the next step in her journey to fulfillment, an adventure that would take her deeper into the unknown and into the realm of her own mind.

The appointment with Woodfire finally arrived, and her sister Honey was there with her, but sadly Maple's consultation with the prestigious psychiatrist had left her with a diagnosis she didn't expect. The doctor believed she might be experiencing bipolar disorder, a condition characterized by mood swings between periods of depression and mania. While Maple was absolutely certain that her experiences weren't due to a mental health condition, she couldn't shake the memory of Jonah's struggle with mental health.

The truth is that Maple was terrified that Jonah's story would be repeated, so she agreed to be medicated. Woodfire prescribed a plan to try to stabilize her mood and "alleviate" those symptoms she had described, including the voices in her head.

Honey took Maple to her apartment, but not before stopping by the pharmacy to pick up the pills Woodfire had prescribed. Honey herself read the boxes and labels of the pills and gave her Maple ones she had to take. Maple took them in her hands. She couldn't help but feel conflicted. On the one hand, she wanted to trust the evaluation of this handsome doctor and was willing to do whatever it took to ensure her well-being. But on the other hand, she had a deep conviction that her experiences were not rooted in mental illness, but, in fact, were a real and magical connection to Mister Universe.

Maple understood that she had to find a balance between medical treatment and her truly amazing and unique experience. In the depths of her heart, she hoped that the medication would provide her with some clarity while also allowing her to explore the mysteries of "10:25" and her connection to Mister Universe.

Days passed and then weeks, and the voices in her head were getting lower and lower and the most discouraging thing of all was that the medication was also affecting her mood, She couldn't get answers to all those doubts she had found on her life's path, but she hoped that, in spite of everything, Mister Universe would bring her closer to the answers she was looking for.

As Maple adjusted to the medication, though faintly, the experiences and symbolism of her magic-filled adventure continued to play an important role in her thoughts. For her, the mysteries of her connection to Mister Universe were far from gone, and she knew she had to prove to Honey, the doctors, and everyone else that everything she had experienced was true.

Chapter 20: Magic Has Vanished

The medication began to take effect in her mind. The voices were suddenly quieter. It was as if Mister Universe had disconnected the lines that connected Maple directly to him and all of his magic. With the voices fading, so did the joy and wonder that had managed to make her life more magnificent.

Maple found herself in a state of emotional numbness. The pills, meant to stabilize her mood, had also turned off her senses, her emotions, and the saddest thing, they had also turned off her ability to connect with Mister Universe. Maple's life once again felt dull and joyless, and she couldn't help but mourn the loss of that vibrant, magical world she had once been a part of.

Despite the effects of the medication, memories of her amazing adventure were scattered throughout her apartment. The peacock feathers, collected during her walk through Marina Willows, were still as vibrant and beautiful as when she found them. Each feather was a validation of her unique and real connection to Mister Universe.

That rock she had found in Cuervo Hills, that rock beautifully adorned with the image of the unnumbered card was still resting on her shelf full of books, it was like a physical representation of the mysteries she had found, one more clue in Mister Universe's incredible game. All those memories kept the flame of her beliefs in everything she had experienced alive, even if it was only a game crafted by her brain.

Maple longed for the return of those voices in her head, the magic and wonder they had brought to her once sad life. She felt conflicted about the medication, torn between the desire to continue living in the midst of magic and the logical need for emotional stability.

The mysteries of "10:25" were still present in her drowsy head. Since Maple started taking her medication, her life had become a mundane and joyless existence and the voices that had taken her on so many adventures had dimmed, leaving her feeling disconnected from the ordinary world. Although the pills were designed to stabilize her mood, they had left her in a state of depression, a stark contrast to the happiness she had once looked straight in the eye.

Maple and Ria's apartment, while filled with vibrant peacock feathers, beautifully painted rocks, and other symbols of her adventure, now felt like a real prison. Maple rarely left her apartment and had begun to isolate herself from the world more and more. Pancake, her faithful dog, was her only constant companion, and she often spoke to him as if he would one day respond.

Ria, her quiet, introverted roommate, was also there, but their interactions were limited, because of Ria struggling with social interactions. Maple's Loneliness was palpable, and the lack of a real human bond had left her adrift in a sea of depression.

Maple's thoughts were often about the pills that left her feeling like a zombie and the diagnosis she had received. Was it really possible that she was bipolar, or had she been misdiagnosed? Maple wondered if her medication was causing more harm than good. The side effects, including weight gain, only added to her frustration.

Maple had struggled with weight all her life, and the ups and downs had always been a source of emotional pain, and the medication was only making it worse.

As the days turned into weeks, and Maple's world grew smaller, the walls of her apartment seemed to be closing in on her. She longed for the return of the magic and wonder that had once defined her life. The mysteries of "10:25" and her connection to Mister Universe were still waiting to be explored, but the medication had left her in a state of emotional numbness.

Pancake was her only confidant, and Maple vented to him. She dreamed of finding some way to break free from the sparkless existence that had gripped her and determined to find a way back to the vibrant, magical world that had once defined her life, even if it meant reevaluating her diagnosis and the pills she had been prescribed.

Chapter 21: My Best Friend, Julie Goldbucket

In the midst of the dull and joyless days of Maple's life since taking her pills, there was one lifeline that kept her afloat: her unbreakable friendship with Julie. Julie's demanding job as a senior marketing consultant and her commitment to her fiancé, Sam, left her with limited free time. However, the moments they spent together during their "girls' nights"–watching their favorite show "Race for Fashion", drinking Carmenere wine or delicious apple Martinis–were the highlight of the week for Maple.

Those nights offered Maple a respite from the isolation and depression she was drowning in, making her feel alive again, at least for a few hours once a week. Their laughter, conversations, and camaraderie reminded her of the good things in life beyond her medication and the confines of her apartment.

Julie had an exciting career, and her life was busy. She was a source of inspiration for Maple. Her strength as a woman in the business world had always been an inspiration for what could be achieved in this life through hard work and determination, and Maple admired her for it.

Julie's fiancé, Sam, took up much of Julie's time. Their relationship was undoubtedly complex. Julie loved him, and they had dated for years, but their relationship lacked the depth and passion Julie deserved.

Despite the uncertainties in her own life, Maple had always been a source of support and advice for Julie, always offering her a listening ear and her valuable perspectives, always optimistic.

Maple really valued her incredible friendship with Julie and all the moments they had shared since childhood. It was during those moments with Julie that Maple felt a spark of happiness and that the magic that had once defined her life still existed. The mysteries of "10:25" and its connection to Mister Universe remained there, but in the background, waiting for the opportunity to be explored once again.

Amid her struggles with medication and the weight of her bipolar diagnosis, Julie's friendship was a beacon of hope and proof that she could still find joy in this world. Maple knew that, with Julie by her side, she could overcome the challenges ahead and rediscover the magic that had once filled her life.

Chapter 22: Pearl's Advice

Maple was feeling the weight of her depression and that overwhelming sense of isolation. Though she felt somewhat reluctant for some reason, she decided to reach out to her mother, Pearl, anyway. Throughout her life, in those moments of despair, Pearl had always known exactly what to say to bring comfort and peace.

Maple confided all the things that were going on in her life to her mother, the attenuation of her experiences with Mister Universe, Haja Island, the mystery of "10:25", her weight gain thanks to those antipsychotic pills she was taking and above all the overwhelming feeling of lack of joy, Pearl listened attentively with all the empathy and understanding that Maple needed. Honey had already shared her side of Maple's story with her mother, but while Pearl tried not to judge anyone, she certainly had her own perspective on the whole situation.

Pearl had always been a gentle soul and an empathetic listener. She was really scared of what might be happening to her daughter, and she had to be careful about how she would deal with the situation. Pearl dug deep within herself for the most adequate words and suggested that Maple consider leaving her apartment more. She believed that a change in her surroundings and fresh air might help alleviate some of her depression and the horrible isolation that had gripped her. The wise words of Pearl showed the unwavering support she had for her daughter, even if they didn't always talk on the phone or visit each other.

Honey had always been more pragmatic in her approach, and it was absolutely necessary for her that Maple keep taking her pills. Her direct and realistic nature had led her to believe that medication was the only right way for her sister's recovery. Maple felt caught between the different opinions of her closest family.

That advice to get out of her apartment more just made a lot of sense, and it was hard for Maple to deny the comfort she felt talking to her mother. Despite all the differences they might have had, Maple knew that no matter what challenges she faced, she could always count on the support and love of her family, including Honey.

In the midst of the struggles that were battling inside her head, Maple tried to remind herself of the importance of her family and the role her mother and sister played in her life. She just had to find some way to navigate the complexities of her unique experience and rediscover the magic that had once filled her world. It still had to exist somewhere.

Taking her mother's advice to heart, Maple decided to leave her apartment to take a short walk and breathe in the fresh air once again. Her favorite place on Earth, Marina Willows, had always been a source of peace and inspiration. It was home to the Serengeti and Cuervo Hills, names Maple had invented during her many hikes and adventures in the park.

As she ventured through the intertwined paths of Marina Willows, Maple felt something powerful, a comforting sensation that flooded the foundations of her being.

The lush vegetation, the tranquility that she could find in the most secluded corners of the gigantic park, those hidden corners full of untamed natural beauty that had always held a special place in her dreamy heart. Despite the challenges that insisted on being a part of her life, this place full of magic was still a constant source of inspiration.

The Serengeti, that part of the park that Maple had affectionately named after the African plains, was an open space in Marina Willows full of majestic rocky hills where she and her beloved dog Pancake had lived countless carefree moments full of plenitude in connection with the beauty of nature. It reminded her of the documentaries she used to watch with her father Roman when she was just a child. These documentaries that played on television during weekends had always stirred amazement in Maple, who deeply admired the beauty of the animal kingdom.

Cuervo Hills, that place where she had found that rock meticulously decorated with the mysterious message, was undoubtedly a place full of memories and secrets that were anxiously waiting to be unraveled. As Maple walked among the rocks of Cuervo Hills, Marina Willows' crows followed her intently, and Maple could feel the weight of her depression was gradually fading away. All that natural beauty, the singing of the birds and the soft rustling of the leaves in the wind, rekindled that sense of wonder she felt as a child, despite all the pain that came with her childhood. It was as if the park itself whispered in her ear, encouraging her to enjoy the world despite the negative effects of her medication.

With each step Maple took, she kept thinking about the relevance of "10:25" and Mister Universe, of course...
How could she forget it? Marina Willows, on the other hand, had always been a place where magic and inspiration thrived, and she knew that, by returning to her sanctuary, she was taking a significant step toward rediscovering the pure and absolute happiness that for a brief moment had defined her life. That happiness she had found belonged to her and neither the pills nor anyone else were going to take it away from her.

Chapter 23: The Cards Have Spoken

There in her sanctuary, Marina Willows, Maple decided that she wanted to reconnect with the magic of her cards, and decided to draw three from her deck, that same deck that she had painstakingly crafted through an unknown inspiration to represent various aspects of life, love, and all aspects of Mister Universe's cosmic game. These beautiful cards had already guided her through a labyrinth full of symbolism and amazingly hidden messages. But now, they had an even more special meaning, one that transcended the voices she had once heard in her head.

The first card she drew from her mysterious divination deck was card number seven: "The Forgotten Lighthouse." Maple had learned to read these cards inspired by the knowledge that had been transmitted to her by Mister Universe, this specific card was a symbol of guidance and enlightenment, but it was also a reminder that sometimes we lose sight of our own destiny. This lighthouse that had once guided ships safely to shore, was now forgotten, as was Maple's magical connection to the mysteries of "10:25."

Maple proceeded to randomly choose a second card, the card she drew was number 28: "The Lunatic", this card undoubtedly reflected her own experiences, her own adventure on the paths of existence and represented the idea that, sometimes, what others perceived as madness was, in fact, a unique and unconventional form of ancestral wisdom. It was a clue that encouraged Maple to embrace her individuality and the magic of her experiences, even if it seemed unconventional to those around her. Crazy actually meant happy.

With excitement, she proceeded to take the third card, closed her eyes, and when she opened them he saw that the lucky card was number 67: "The lost key", this card had a beautiful design of an ancient key decorated with flowers and thorns on its front, its meaning spoke of something missing or something hidden, a puzzle perhaps, waiting to be put together. Although Maple felt disconnected and depressed, this card seemed to tell her that there were mysteries to unravel and clues to uncover, both within herself and in the world around her, and this seemed to temper those feelings of depression and disappointment.

The voices Maple used to hear in her head had faded, perhaps not entirely, but amazingly, Maple's connection to her cards seemed to be alive and well. These enigmatic cards, once only a source of guidance and hidden messages, as a form of wholesome entertainment, now offered her a different kind of relief. There was still meaning and purpose in Maple Pelridge's life, even when the world seemed bleak and unhappy.

Maple deeply contemplated the meaning of these three cards, she understood that they contained messages that transcended the need for the voices in her head, after all, Maple believed that Mister Universe had been the magical inspiration behind them, even before she had seen his colossal eyes in front of the ocean. Marina Willows, which was her sanctuary of inspiration, was again that place where she managed to feel a new ray of hope shine within her being, where she managed to feel a sense that the magic and illusion she had once known could still find their way back into her life.

Chapter 24: Darkness

Haja Island, which for some time was a place of charm and mystery, had been absent from Maple's recent adventures. The very idea of the magic that surrounded the island had now become a source of deep sadness and longing for those moments when Maple had known true happiness. It was becoming increasingly clear to Maple that her medication was restricting her, preventing her from being her true self, and clearly shutting down all the magic that had once filled her life.

The wisdom-filled voices that Maple had heard in her head, which had guided her to so many magical places and unique experiences, were now shrouded in a terrifying silence. Those ridiculously amazing messages that had connected her to the torturous riddle of "10:25" and, of course, the wise Mister Universe had now disappeared, leaving her longing for the sense of wonder and purpose that had come with the adventure of self-discovery.

The pills Maple was taking had brought with them their own form of emotional isolation and seemed to unsharpen her senses and obscure the vibrant colors that had once made her life awesome. Maple undoubtedly missed those days when she was in total harmony with the world around her, when those voices she heard in her head guided her and shared their ancestral wisdom.

The world had now become a dull place for Maple, one where magic seemed distant and elusive. Maple longed for the return of that magical charm present in Mister Universe's games, those that once transformed her life forever, that connection to something as immense as the power of her dreams.

Maple continued to walk through Marina Willows Park, in the absence of those voices that had once spoken to her. She was determined to find her way back to the enchantment she had once known, a longing that burned within her, that fervent desire to rediscover the magic that had once been an essential part of her very being.

Maple often found herself pondering the small, velvety white berry that had set off an incredible series of events full of magic. In her lonely head dwelt a stubborn thought that, perhaps, that utterly innocent-looking berry was the key to everything: the voices in her head, all those hidden clues, the golden symbols, Haja Island, and even Mister Universe himself.

That berry was curiously different from any other Maple had ever tasted, tasting so little in just a tiny bite. Maple had crossed an enchanted bridge to other worlds. Eating an unknown berry from the Fairy Forest had been an undeniably risky experience, consuming it could have literally killed Maple.

Maple thought about how that invisible hand pushed her to venture into the fairy forest, where those voices had begun to guide her on a mystical journey that defied all rational explanations.

That berry had apparently been the catalyst, the spark that ignited the amazing chain of events that had forever transformed Maple's perception of reality.

Among the doubts circling in her head, she couldn't help but wonder if there was something inherently magical about that berry, something that might have activated a connection to the secrets of "10:25" and the Hidden Order that Maple had eventually found thanks to the voices of wisdom echoing in her head. Could that mysterious berry contain the answers to the questions that had filled her mind since everything began?

Maple continued to contemplate the meaning of that velvety white berry non-stop, the sense of curiosity and determination was constantly welling up within her being. It was as if a new purpose had ignited within her, an expedition to unearth the truth about that little fruit and especially its role in her incredible and unlikely adventure.

With each passing day, the mystery surrounding that gorgeously white berry became more and more enticing, and Maple couldn't shake the feeling that it was a clue from Mister Universe so she could unravel the secrets that had eluded her for so long. It was a search that would take her deeper into the realms of the unknown, where the ordinary and the extraordinary converged, and where those voices in her head might perhaps guide her once more on her path full of magical revelations.

Chapter 25: Return to the Fairy Forest

Despite the numbing effects of her medication, a nagging urge tugged at Maple's heart, an impulse that called her by name to that magical place where her extraordinary adventure had apparently begun: the Fairy Forest, deep in Marina Willows Park. It was there that she was determined to find that elusive little velvety white berry that looked like a tiny peach. Maple couldn't get the thought out of her head that, that berry had been the catalyst for the magical events that followed.

While it was true that the pills might have desensitized her senses, they were not able to suppress the curiosity that had been awoken inside Maple, who fervently longed to see that seemingly enchanted berry again, to examine it and understand how something so tiny could have opened the doors to a world full of magic and amazing wonders.

The thought of tasting the berry again frightened her greatly, since consuming it that time had set in motion a sequence of events that were far beyond her comprehension. But Maple's innate curiosity overcame her fears and apprehension. The need to hold that enigmatic berry in her hands, feel its texture, examine its seemingly innocent velvety exterior and sweet, juicy pulp had led her to extraordinary discoveries that surpassed science fiction.

Maple was in her apartment, sharing her thoughts with her dog Pancake, who, although was not able to speak, offered her his innocent and curious stare, when she saw him in the eyes Maple remembered the importance of her mission, so she headed towards Marina Willows. As she walked deeper into the Fairy Forest, she tried to retrace that winding path that had once led her to that bush full of magical berries. In some strange way, it was as if the forest itself recognized her presence and gave her a warm welcome to this mythical place where the line between reality and magic had blurred.

The voices Maple used to hear in her head, though distant, seemed to whisper softly, as if they were encouraging her in her quest. At that moment, Maple could not deny the possibility that the mysteries of "10:25" and the Hidden Order were perhaps intertwined with the very essence of this place that seemed to be a portal to another world.

Maple's heart raced with each step that brought her closer to the spot where the enchanted berry had first caught her attention. Maple closed her eyes. Suddenly the tiny white berry, soft as velvet, lay before her, innocent and unpretentious. Maple slowly approached that bush that seemed to tell her to take another step. Step-by-step, Maple found herself standing in front of the bush, examining it with a mixture of fascination and uneasiness.

As she held the velvety berry in her hands, she was strangely captivated by the power within, the power of unlocking a world of magic within her being, the power to connect her to the magnificent Mister Universe.

Maple knew that this elusive berry was more powerful than it appeared to be, and it was undoubtedly the key to understanding the incredible magical adventure that had decorated her days.

Maple rubbed the delicate exterior of the berry with her fingers, felt the fuzz caressing her senses, and a renewed sense of purpose grew deep within her. That quest to unravel the enchanting mysteries of her adventure had only just begun, and she was eager to discover the truth behind its magical properties. The Fairy Forest was undoubtedly a special place full of wonder and connection to something grander, and it held the promise of answers that had long eluded her. Maple opened her eyes.

Maple's heart was pounding fast, set to find that magical berry bush she remembered so vividly from just a few seconds ago. That same glittering berry she had tasted that threw her down a slide beyond her wildest imagination, and she was determined to retrace her steps, even if she had to walk in circles a thousand times, in order to discover more about the extraordinarily powerful berries. Maple walked and walked along the intertwining paths. However, when she reached the spot where she firmly believed the bushes should have been, she was met with a disconcerting sight: the elusive enchanted bush was nowhere to be found.

She stood there, staring at the empty space where the bushes should have been, her heart swollen with confusion. She knew that those berries were as real as life itself; She had tasted its delicious magic and navigated the deep waters of absolute power.

But now, the very elusive berries had disappeared without a trace, leaving her with yet another enigma with no clear answers.

It was as if Mister Universe himself had played another mean joke on her, erasing the very source of her fantastic adventures. Maple felt frustrated and helpless once again. How was it possible that something so important in her destiny simply disappeared?

The voices in remained silent, offering no guidance or explanation. It was a discouraging moment for Maple. Without a doubt, she was hopeful that she would see the berry bushes, and this was going to give her some clarity about the mysterious journey she had undertaken.

Maple continued to search all around, her determination remained unwavering, and she was unwilling for any reason to accept that the berries and magic she had experienced were mere figments of her imagination. There had to be some explanation, some way to understand why the berries had vanished, eluding her.

Chapter 26: Home Sweet Home

Disappointed, Maple decides to return to her apartment, when she opens the door her eyes swept the room, looking at her precious belongings, each of which held a special place in her heart and was part of a unique connection to her past and to Mister Universe. The apartment she shared with Ria was a trunk filled with memories and treasures, a sanctuary that provided comfort and peace in times of confusion and uncertainty.

Maple took small steps as she admired her amazing collection of beautifully detailed maps of unknown islands. Each of those anonymous islands was a world waiting to be explored by Maple's dreamy heart, who imagined the majestic landscapes that adorned them. Those maps promised her adventures, turning on the light bulb in her imagination, reminding her that life's possibilities were limitless.

Photographs of Maple's chosen family were scattered throughout the apartment: a photo of her and Honey as children on the beach, a photo of her parents, Pearl and Roman when they were still married, A black-and-white photo of her mother when she was just a child, another photo with her father with a glass of wine in the countryside a few years before he left this life, a series of snapshots of her on her adventures with Julie and another truly special photo of the whole family together, captured in a moment of pure bliss. Each image was a symbol of the incredible relationships that had shaped her life.

In one corner was an altar that Maple had decorated with shells, semi-precious stones she had found in her adventures, various figurines of imaginary gods and goddesses, made of clay and sand by Maple herself. That humble altar was a place of contemplation and reflection for Maple's dreaming heart. It was a space where she found comfort and a sense of spiritual connection and peace.

A beautiful selection of painstakingly painted rocks adorned different corners of her home. Each of them had been painted with love, their designs divinely inspired by nature and the golden alien symbols that had captivated her for a while. Her creativity was nothing more than a tangible product of all those wonders that she carried within her being to share with the world around her.

The floating shelves displayed a wide variety of figurines, from wooden dinosaurs to a small woolly llama souvenir of her trip to Peru with Jonah. These little memories spoke of her adventures and experiences that she had accumulated along the way. They were undoubtedly whimsical souvenirs of the joyful moments she had shared with a special person who had once occupied an important place in her life.

Maple contemplated every corner of her apartment. Surrounded by the physical representations of her past and the experiences that had defined her, she found a sense of prosperity and belonging. Her home was a painting of her journey, a journey that had been filled with moments of magic, adventure, and connection.

While the mysteries of her life still hung over her, the familiarity of her home provided her with a sense of groundedness and tranquility. Maple understood that her quest for understanding was bound to continue, but for now, she could take comfort in the tangible reminders of the experiences that had made her the person she had become, a person proud of who she was.

As Maple continued to wander around her apartment, she observed the patterns and routines that made up her daily life. Pancake, her son, the most beautiful dog, the light of her eyes, slept peacefully, curled up next to Ria, her roommate. Ria had just returned from her day at the library, a job she certainly loved but often left her feeling exhausted by the constant interaction with people, who overwhelmed her.

Ria's routine was simple but comforting. She had adapted to her own slow pace: she would diligently prepare her favorite noodle soups, retire to her room for a while, and then come back out to tackle the dishes. This cycle was like a comforting anchor in her daily life, providing her with a sense of structure and predictability.

Maple's apartment was undoubtedly a welcoming environment for Ria, who often practiced her relaxing yoga poses in front of the TV. These moments of solitude and movement were what allowed her to reconnect with herself and find her inner peace, a precious respite from the demands of her mentally exhausting work.

A small gray couch by the window was the perfect place for Ria to take occasional naps. Those brief breaths allowed her to recharge her batteries and face the world with renewed energy.

As Maple looked intently at the confines of her apartment, she couldn't help but feel gratitude for the stable, comforting environment she had created and both she and Ria could enjoy.

Although incredible mysteries and magical adventures had filled her life, the routines of everyday existence provided her with peace and refuge.

Maple continued walking slowly down the narrow corridor that separated the kitchen from the bedrooms, suddenly stopping to see a magnificent painting that decorated one of the walls opposite Ria's room. This majestic work of art that Maple had created during one of her "episodes" was born out of her creative spirit and was so beautiful that it had become a source of endless fascination for her own creative talents. On the huge canvas, an intricate combination of vibrant colors unfolded: deep yellows and blues, with strokes of golden paint intertwined in horizontal and vertical brushstrokes of various shapes and sizes, each painted with meticulous attention, despite being completely abstract, infinite minute details were hidden within the complexity of the magnificent composition.

But what made this painting truly captivating was its ability to reveal hidden treasures to anyone who gazed at it for more than a second.

Maple herself often found herself caught up in its riddles, getting lost in the ever-changing patterns and shifting tones. The longer you stared at the painting, the more it seemed to reveal bright colors, from delicate shades of pinks and purples to vibrant blues and greens, accompanied by warm yellows and oranges. It was like a party for the eyes, a truly captivating spectacle that revealed something new every time it was observed.

As Maple continued to gaze at the painting, she felt an

undeniable attraction to its mesmerizing beauty: it was as if it reflected her inner world, as if it were a celebration of her creativity and the limitless possibilities that life had to offer.

A mirror with a wooden frame, beautifully carved with Victorian floral designs, hung right in front of the magnificent painting. Maple turned and was awestruck by her own reflection. In that seemingly ordinary mirror, she observed every detail of her reflection and, in a voice full of conviction, she uttered the following words of affirmation. "You are truly beautiful, inside and out," a brief silence interrupted her, and she went on to say, "You deserve to see each of your dreams come true. You will become that famous influencer you are destined to be. You will leave an indelible mark on this world."

Her beloved mirror had become a portal to her dreams, echoing her illusions and her deepest aspirations.

It was the purest moment of self-love and empowerment, a memo that reminded her that she had all the potential to shape her destiny and manifest her dreams.

Maple's intimate interaction with her reflection helped her find within herself the strength and confidence to achieve the goals she had set for herself, despite the mysteries and challenges that always loomed ahead. That humble apartment was not only a place where she felt comfortable or safe, but was also a constant source of inspiration, a place where she could reaffirm her own worth and believe in the endless possibilities that awaited her.

Maple stood in front of Ria's door and thanked Mister Universe for finding such a charming and authentic person as Ria to be her roommate. Finally, she entered her room. She gently closed the door, allowing a sense of absolute freedom to envelop her. The inside of her room was a truly cozy retreat, where the complexities of the outside world seemed to fade away and where the whispers of her thoughts could be heard most clearly.

She turned on the light, automatically; her gaze focused on a framed puzzle hanging from the brick wall. It was none other than the enigmatic Mister Pancake, her beloved dog. This puzzle was a prized possession, a Christmas present for herself a few years ago. She remembered putting it together with Jonah piece by piece. That puzzle was a physical representation of the special bond she shared with her everything, her very life, the source of her joy, her great love, Pancake.

Just below the puzzle lay her queen-size bed, the place where her most sublime dreams were born. That comfortable bed spoke to her in sign language through its soft pillows and pleasant blankets, inviting her to relax and unwind, where dreams and memories intertwined, where her thoughts could wander freely in the quiet hours of the night.

Maple's room was a sanctuary within a sanctuary, a place where she could escape the outside world and explore the inner landscapes of her mind. In that room, she found a respite from the mysteries and challenges she constantly faced in her life; it was a space where her inner voice could speak freely, a place where her dreams could take shape and where she could nurture her connection with the enigmatic Mister Universe.

Here, in the comfort of her room, Maple could embrace the whispers of her heart, ponder the mysteries of her existence, and contemplate the adventures that awaited her beyond the confines of the walls.

Chapter 27: Open Your Eyes

Maple was lying on her comfortable bed, with Pancake curled up next to her. Maple held her phone in her hand, incredulous. Her thoughts were mired in the crowd of notifications flooding her screen, the sheer number of alerts was ridiculously staggering, it seemed impossible, which made her wonder what could have happened, she couldn't shake the feeling that someone might have had some kind of accident or something. The truth is that she had no idea what had happened to have so many notifications. After all, Maple no longer enjoyed any magical power since she started her antipsychotic treatment.

She felt curious and agitated, but she drew courage from within her being and opened her social media app, and as the reality of what had happened unfolded before her, a sense of disbelief came over her. It was as if the world had changed, or perhaps she was as crazy as she thought she was. This was something that totally challenged her understanding of reality. Was what her eyes saw true, or was it just another cruel joke in her frail existence? Maple's mind teetered on the edge of the precipice of skepticism and wonder.

She closed her eyes and let herself be enveloped by mandalas swirling in violet tones that danced in her mind. Maple wanted to make contact with those voices that had fallen silent, those ethereal whispers that seemed to have retreated into the recesses of her consciousness.

When she least expected it, a rather unique and familiar voice answered her inner question. "Maple, I never abandoned you," and then he said. "Open your eyes."

Maple took a deep breath, allowing her eyelids to slowly open, and turned her gaze once more to her phone, trying to absorb that incredible revelation that seemed to want to shake her understanding of the world and her place in it.

Maple's heartbeat raced as she stared at her phone screen, disbelief washing over her in waves. It seemed that one of her videos, a simple moment captured in Marina Willows with Pancake, had undergone a truly dramatic transformation. That innocent video had apparently gone viral, accumulating millions of "likes" and millions of views, numbers that seemed to rise with each passing second. The realization was almost surreal. It was a tremendous contrast to the modest audience she was used to.

Her mind seemed to burst from so many questions and emotions she was feeling as she dealt with this sudden surge of attention. How on Earth had this happened? Could this be real? What did it mean for her future, for those almost impossible dreams of making a real impact on the world?

Maple honestly wasn't able to believe anything that was going on. She closed her eyes and again saw those purple mandalas dancing inside her mind. She spoke again to those mysterious voices that had guided her in the past, seeking their infinite wisdom.

An important question hung in the air, a question that echoed within herself: "Will I finally achieve all the personal success I deserve? Is this my chance to make this world a better place?"

A silence lingered in her mind, which only made her anticipation worse. Out of nowhere, she heard a whisper from Mister Universe himself, who responded with words that resonated deeply in her being: "Don't forget rule number one."

With those words echoing in her thoughts, Maple contemplated the new opportunity that had arisen in her life. Her adventure was taking a surprising turn, and in order to face this new chapter of her life, she had to keep alive the essence of joy, optimism, and the belief that she could achieve anything she wanted in her passage through this world, step by step.

Her heart was brimming with excitement and hope, Maple didn't yet know that this sudden viral hit wasn't just an isolated incident. The impact had spread like wildfire through all of her videos, and her audience seemed to grow at a truly astounding rate. It was as if Mister Universe had conspired to grant her the platform she had always dreamed of.

It wasn't just about the numbers, the likes, or the views. It was about the opportunity to share her message, to spread love, positivity and inspire meaningful change in the world, and most importantly, to use her platform to denounce animal abuse in all its forms, help people open their eyes and understand that the animals were here with us and not for us. Maple was a dreamer and had always believed in the power of optimism, truth, and love.

Now, she had the stage to make a real difference, one smile at a time.

With every video she created, and every message she shared, she had the ability to make her mark on the world. In this exciting new chapter of her life, she would always remember "rule number one": have fun, enjoy the ride, and seize every moment with love and optimism. Maple's heart was filled with gratitude for the unexpected turn her life had taken. She finally felt truly ready to face the world and fulfill her dreams, knowing that Mister Universe had a plan for her, and she was finally on the path to her dreams.

Chapter 28: The Voices

The next day, after waking up from the best sleep she had ever had, Maple scrupulously looked at the two cards she had drawn from her divination deck. The first card, "Mister Universe," undoubtedly had immense meaning for her. It was a symbol of the deep connection she shared with this being of higher power, that enigmatic voice at the edge of the ocean with eyes as bright as those of a cat. This card represented the beginning of her amazing adventure, a path that had transported her to a world soaked in magic and mystery.

The second card, "The Dunes of Time," reminded Maple of the importance of time and the flow of life. It encouraged her to appreciate the past, to live in the present, and to look to the future. The dunes symbolized the ever-changing nature of time and the quicksand that were the foundations of her own life.

Maple held these cards in her hands, they revealed to her that her magical adventure was far from over. She was finally beginning to uncover Mister Universe's secrets and the mysteries that had been hidden for so long. The guidance of her divination cards and her growing online community inspired her to embrace the adventure that awaited her with open arms.

A renewed sense of purpose and determination was pulsating fiercely within Maple. she wasn't just creating content; She was sharing her own magic, her wisdom, and her love with the world. As she looked at her cards, she was filled with a deep sense of gratitude.

Maple sat down at her desk. Her cards were spread out in front of her. She needed inspiration for her next video, one that would resonate with her growing online community and carry a meaningful message of hope, love, and positivity.

She took her cards and shuffled them while silently praying to Mister Universe. As she arranged the cards, she felt a deep connection to the symbolism that they had within, as if they were guiding her in the right direction. The first card she drew was "The Blooming Lotus", it represented growth, transformation and the silent power of nature's beauty in difficult circumstances. It was the perfect card to represent her magnificent adventure and the message she wanted to convey to her new followers.

Maple didn't know exactly what her next video would be about. But she wanted to share details of her personal transformation, her struggles, and her battle to find her true self. It would be a video full of authenticity, vulnerability, and the strength that came from her magic-filled experiences, which filled her with a new sense of purpose, Maple began writing the script for her video, putting her heart and soul into every word. She wanted her viewers to know that they were not alone in their struggles, that there was always hope, and that the journey to self-discovery could lead to a beautiful and fulfilling life.

As she worked on her video, the voices inside her head remained silent, but Maple felt their presence in the wisdom and clarity she had gained throughout her extraordinary spiritual process.

This video was more than just content; It was a validation of the power of optimism, resilience, and an unwavering belief in the magic of life.

Maple pondered this for a moment and realized that while sharing her personal experience and struggles was important, she had a unique connection to the mysterious Haja Island and the clues she received from "Mister Universe." This was something extraordinary, a secret that had the potential to inspire and surprise her followers even more.

As she considered her options, she thought about the meaning of the second card she had drawn from her deck, "The Dunes of Time." This card represented the concept of time as a vast and ever-changing landscape and reminded her that there were endless stories to tell.

Maple decided to take a slightly different approach. For her next video. Instead of sharing her personal experience, she would delve into the mysteries of time, consciousness, and the unseen forces that guide our lives. She would create a video that would explore the interconnectedness of all living things, the beauty of the universe, and the magic that existed in the most ordinary moments.

This video would be inspired by the transformative magic of Haja Island and would be a celebration of the unique bond that bound her to "Mister Universe". Maple believed that her divine inspiration would distinguish her in the world of online influencers.

Maple began planning and writing the script for her new video, drawing inspiration from her own experiences and the hidden messages she had received. It would be a video like no other, and it

would carry a powerful message of unity, hope, and life's limitless
possibilities.

Chapter 29: Magic is Alive and Well

Maple walked toward Marina Willows in the soft glow of the park's lights, carrying her container with leftover food. Maple had always been fascinated by crows, with their intelligence and enigmatic presence. Although she had been warned about the "don't feed the birds" policy, she decided to ignore it that night. She wanted to share a special moment with these wonderfully wise creatures who had become her inseparable companions during her incredible magical adventures.

Maple whistled that tune she always whistled when she visited Cuervo Hills. The crows came out of nowhere from among the twisted branches of the oak trees and began to congregate, attracted by the promise of the food that Maple had brought. Seeing all the excited crows perched around her, she scattered the leftovers on the ground and the birds began to feast. It was a truly hypnotic sight to see how they rummaged through the morsels that Maple gave them. Their magnificent black feathers shone under the soft artificial light, creating an almost surreal scene.

For Maple, that moment, that simple act of kindness had the power to create a unique and captivating video. The incredibly powerful connection that exists between humans and nature, that implicit connection she felt with crows and that drew joy on her face when she saw them feed. All this would be the subject of her next video.

Maple grabbed her phone and began recording the beauty of the crows eating and the serenity of the park at night. Maple was aware that this video would be different from the previous ones, perhaps not achieving the same success as her other viral videos, but she felt it was the right way to express her gratitude for the unexpected success she had experienced.

The video was beginning to come to life on her screen. She couldn't contain her smile. Her sense of purpose was more alive than ever. Although her adventure had taken many unexpected turns, at the end of the day, it was taking her to a place where her passion for nature, and the infinite power of love could make a real difference in the world and prove that yes, magic was real.

Maple believed in Mister Universe's magic firmly, and now, she was finally ready to share that magic with the world. This video was just the beginning of her new mission, one in which she would continue to pursue her dreams and create truly magical content for all who saw it.

Feeling satisfied with the video she had recorded, she left the park, hoping that her video would touch the hearts of many. Upon returning to her apartment, she couldn't wait to share this special moment with Julie, her closest confidant, and see how the world would respond to her new inspiration.

Maple's apartment was bathed in the soft moonlight filtering through the kitchen windows, creating a serene atmosphere. Maple watched over the sleep of Pancake, her faithful companion, who was curled up in his cozy blanket, snoring as if there was no tomorrow. She came over and gently stroked his head. Pancake woke up full of joy and licked her whole face.

Maple had a lot of things on her head, including Pancake's saliva. Those voices to which Maple opened the doors of her soul had taken her on an extraordinary journey, full of mysteries and discoveries. She wasn't entirely sure if they were real or just figments of her imagination, but she knew one thing for sure: this new chapter of her life would be as full of adventure and excitement as those moments when she immersed herself in the enchanting magic of Mister Universe.

As she got ready for bed, Maple kept thinking about her next video, the one she had shot earlier at Marina Willows Park. It was an interesting departure from her usual content, a glimpse into her deep connection to crows and nature's charms.

She climbed onto her bed, looked at Mister Pancake's framed puzzle, and a whirlwind of emotions grew in her mind. Out of nowhere Maple closed her eyes, glad to know that she was on the cusp of something extraordinary, something that would not only change her life but also touch the lives of those who followed her on her extraordinary adventure.

Chapter 30: The Eternal Awakening

Maple quickly got used to her newfound social media success. She used her platform to spread a message of love, optimism, and the absolute importance of nature. Her videos were gaining more and more followers and had a real impact. Her new videos showcased her adventures not only in her favorite place, Marina Willows, but eventually all over the world. Her posts showed her infinite love for animals and her sincere messages about life and nature, but above all the importance of understanding that we are in this world to protect and wrap ourselves in the spells of nature, not to abuse it.

Maple could not forget her encounter with Mister Universe, the mysterious voices and magical experiences she had lived on Haja Island. She was still curious about the hidden messages and symbols that Mister Universe left her as clues to his majestic game. She wondered, of course, what the true meaning of 10:25 was. Her inner child longed for those days of adventure and wonder.

One day, while Maple was walking around Marina Willows, as she often did, out of nowhere she decided to make a video in which she would reveal a part of her past and her inner world to her followers. She was finally ready to talk about her connection to Mister Universe, the divination cards, and the mysteries they had helped unravel. The video was titled "The Eternal Awakening.".

In this video, Maple spoke openly about her experiences with what many would call insanity. The enigmatic velvety white berry she had tasted in the Fairy Forest and the "dreams" they had inspired to be born. She showed her viewers the intricately illustrated cards she had crafted and explained their significance in her life.

Mister Universe had warned Maple that sharing her experiences might lead people to believe she had lost her mind, but Maple was willing to take that risk, she didn't really care if people thought she was crazy, maybe she was, and that was perfectly fine.

The response to "The Eternal Awakening" was absolutely overwhelming. Millions of people connected with the magnitude of her story, and many shared their own experiences related to dreams, mysterious symbols, and unexplained phenomena. Her video circled around the world and started a movement of people looking for meaning and a deeper connection in their lives.

Maple continued to make videos that were a mix of her personal growth mission, nature, and her beloved dog, Pancake. She also embraced her role as an influencer with a mission. With the money that began to flow into Maple's accounts, she traveled to various parts of the world to explore and document the beauty of our planet and how we were all connected to it.

Maple stood firm against the injustice faced by enslaved animals in the meat and leather industry. With steadfast determination, and her newfound income, she not only founded but also played a pivotal role in the creation of thousands of shelters for abused animals.

Her activism spread around the world, forcing more than 800 factories in the meat, dairy, and egg industries to pivot to plant-based alternatives, shaking the foundations of a change that was happening right before their eyes.

Maple's sudden fame exploded overnight on a global scale, and Maple didn't waste a second. With the newfound power that her influence had, she began beach cleanup operations on shores around the world, armed with a brave spirit chosen by Mister Universe himself, orchestrating the removal of tons of plastic from the ocean, a feat that echoed the profound impact of her cause.

But Maple's environmental crusade didn't stop there. In a poetic twist, with a simple hashtag, she started a wildflower propagation movement, spreading the seeds of nature's preciousness around the world.

The most significant of Maple Pelridge's many accomplishments was the establishment of Marina Willows National Park, a sanctuary, protected and preserved, intended to be a refuge for generations to come. The beautiful newly designated National Park not only extended the boundaries of the existing park but also began to reforest the surrounding areas that had been used for logging purposes. This New Park would be the first of many to come.

And even though she was still on her medication, Maple felt more alive than ever. She realized that being an influencer wasn't just about the number of followers or likes, but about having a positive impact on the world, and yes, a little wealth.

Her adventure, guided by Mister Universe, had led her to this exciting new life, where she was finally fulfilling her purpose.

Maple Pelridge's existence had gone through a real

transformation, and she finally understood that all those mysteries and wonders that we encounter in our passage through this life were waiting to be discovered and shared with the world, one video at a time.

The end?

Glossary

Maple Pelridge: The protagonist of the story, deeply connected to nature and the universe, on a journey of self-discovery and spiritual awakening.

Honey Pelridge: Maple's sister, concerned about her well-being and actively involved in her life.

Julie Goldbucket: Maple's best friend, who provides support and unique perspectives on her journey.

Dr. Dinorah Goldbucket: Julie's mother, a psychologist who interacts with Maple, who offers perspective and guidance.

Pearl: Maple's mother, with whom she shares a meaningful and emotional connection.

Roman: Maple's father, with whom she shares a significant and emotional connection.

Lars: Maple's stepfather, who inspires Maple to make art.

Doris: Maple's grandmother, who has dementia.

Ria: Maple's introverted and intellectual roommate.
Jonah: Maple's ex-boyfriend, whose presence may still linger in her memories and experiences.

Sam: Julie's fiancé.

Cami: A mysterious voice that communicates with Maple, whose meaning remains enigmatic.

Darwin: A vendor at a fruit stall in the market.

Dr. Woodfire: A prestigious psychiatrist who treats Maple.

Pancake: Maple's Dog.

Bagel: Julie's cat.

Marina Willows: Maple's favorite spot, a huge park on the edge of her city.

Fairy Forest: A nickname Maple came up with for a lush, wooded area of Marina Willows with a charming energy.

The Serengeti: A nickname Maple came up with for a part of Marina Willows, it conjures up images of the African plains in documentaries.

Cuervo Hills: Immersed in the Serengeti, deep in Marina Willows.

Haja Island: An island where Maple can find herself.

Mister Universe: A mysterious and powerful being encountered by Maple, who influences her worldview and beliefs.

Haja: The personification of nature and life.

The Duck Lagoon: A part of Marina Willows, where Maple sees three turtles balancing on a floating log.

Divination Cards: Cards that Maple created herself, used as a spirit guide, playing an important role in her journey.

Sky Water: Maple's favorite musical group.

Notes:

#westisbest

9 781068 972300